CATCH ME A CATCH

SALLY CLEMENTS

Catch Me A Catch

By Sally Clements

Large Print Edition ISBN: 9798775984144

Copyright © 2012 by Sally Clements

LARGE PRINT

For my wonderful, patient family.
Charlie, Davy, Holly and Jenny, and of course, Sam.

ONE

"Damn it!"

Jack Miller's words whipped away from him in the storm's din. Needles of cold rain lashed his face and his biceps burned with the effort of turning the yacht's stainless steel wheel to keep the keel even, as the waves tossed the little craft from side to side. A blast of freezing water doused him, and his jaw muscles twitched. Jack clenched his teeth so hard it hurt. Lightning flashed, lighting the mast in a shower of sparks. He stared at his radar screen. Nothing. The image was gone.

Salt wet hair smacked into his narrowed eyes. He peered across storm tossed waves to flickering lights in the mist, hovering before the faint outline of mountains against darkened clouds. Land at last! But with his electronics fried, he wouldn't make it around the coast to Dun Laoghaire without repairs.

The land's watercolor outline sharpened at his approach. He'd never visited the country his parents had fled, and yet, with its green lushness within sight, a wave of relief broke over him. There was a jetty ahead and he carefully steered towards it and docked. He was finally home.

The wind fell, but the sky was still grey with threatening clouds. He stripped off his soaked oilskins and pulled on a pair of jeans and a tee shirt. Then he sat at his computer, opened his email, and typed.

Part one of hellish journey completed. Have made Ireland.

Yacht needs repair. Call you later.

He pressed send, closed the laptop, and shoved his wallet full of credit cards into his back pocket.

He could barely lift his exhausted arms to tie his yacht to the jetty. His legs' abused muscles tightened in pain as he staggered onto the wooden planks. The lights of a pub, *The Maiden's Arms,* flickered ahead.

I'd love to be in some maiden's arms right now. But before he could settle down with a pint and a plate of hot food he had to see to his boat. Salt-reddened eyes scanned the row of buildings facing the ocean, searching for a chandler.

There. A large, battered and faded sign, *Devine*

Chandlers swung from iron brackets in the wind. Jack strode towards it.

The store's window was stacked with neat rows of ships supplies. His hands cupped his eyes to peer inside. Good. Well-stocked shelves in the back carried the bigger items. He pushed at the door and cursed when it failed to budge.

A man hurrying toward *The Maiden's Arms* slowed as he drew closer. He pointed. "Devine'll be up in the pub." The stranger clutched his raincoat closer to keep out the biting wind. "What with the festival an' all."

"Thanks." Jack followed him. It looked like he'd be getting a pint sooner than he thought.

———

ANNIE DEVINE SHIFTED on the uncomfortable wooden chair, and flicked through the heavy book in front of her. It had been a desperate morning. Three men in a row peppered her with cheesy chat-up lines. It was only just lunchtime and already exhaustion draped around her like a cloak. She sighed. There were thirteen more long days to endure before the matchmaking festival was over, before she could escape her childhood home, and flee back to Dublin. Annie took off the heavy tortoiseshell frames, and pinched the grooves they'd dug into the top of her nose.

"Drink, Annie?" The barman offered from behind the bar.

"I shouldn't, Niall. I need to keep my head clear."

Niall swiped a beer towel over the counter. "Your dad usually has one around lunchtime during the festival, and another just before dinner. After the attention you were getting from Liam Mackey, I reckon you deserve one."

"Ah, okay, I'm stopping for lunch now anyway." She closed the book. "I'll have a Cinzano and lemonade, please."

"Coming up." He turned away to clink ice cubes into a tall glass.

Nothing much happened in Durna except for the annual matchmaking festival. Forty years ago, a group of lonely fishermen started the tradition. They'd advertised in the Dublin newspapers that Durna was holding a two-week festival where serious singles could come to meet a mate. Annie's grandfather was the first matchmaker. Her father the current one. For the first two weeks in September, her grandfather devoted himself to love. He wrote down details of the local bachelors in his large black book, had private meetings with single ladies who wanted to become married ones, and organized dates for potential couples. Each meeting was carefully logged in the book in his copperplate hand. During the festival, dances were held throughout the day, where couples could socialize. It was an innocent remnant of times gone by. One still relevant today, if the numbers that swelled Durna each festival season were anything to go by.

Her father, Bull, had inherited his father's talent. A book full of successful matches proved it. Today, people came from far and wide to be matched. The first thing they did was find the matchmaker's table in the pub. Her father handled it from there. Bull's illness couldn't have come at a worst time. For his only child, and matchmaking heir, anyway.

A dark shadow, cast by a tall figure in the pub's doorway, blocked the murky sunlight. Annie's gaze locked on the stranger, his darkened features in shadow though sunlight outlined his tall, rangy frame. He walked straight up to Niall.

"I'm looking for Devine." His deep voice was husky, like he hadn't used it for a while.

Her skin prickled, the hairs on her arms standing to attention. Blond highlights streaked his tousled brown hair. Highlights that nature, not nurture, had put there. It was too long for him to be a businessman, and his skin was too tanned. This time of year, Durna got its fair share of surfers coming to prostrate themselves on the waves pounding Ireland's west coast, but this guy was no surfer. She'd lay money on it.

Well-defined cheekbones emphasized a long, straight nose. An air of authority flowed from him. Whoever he was, he wasn't to be messed with. The way he carried himself was reminiscent of a gunslinger striding into the saloon looking for someone to shoot.

What's the matter with me? She couldn't avert her gaze. It was as if he were painted in color while everyone else was sketched in black and white. In the past few months of meticulous, almost obsessive application to her business plan, her attention hadn't wavered for a second. Right now, she couldn't even remember her name.

She smoothed her hair back with nervous fingers. It must just be the circumstances. Masquerading as town matchmaker during the festival will do that to a girl.

"There she is." Niall gestured Annie's direction. "Can I get you something?"

"A Guinness."

"I'll bring it over."

The stranger strode towards her. He scanned her head to toe with appreciative sapphire blue eyes. Her body responded to his quick appraisal as if scorched.

"You're Devine?" He had a husky, American drawl. His tee-shirt barely contained broad shoulders, and he topped Niall by a good five inches. "Sorry, I guess I was expecting a man."

"I'm Annie Devine. I get that a lot. People expect a man, and normally they get one."

His eyebrows shot up.

"I mean, normally my father, Bull Devine, would be here. He's run the business forever."

She bit her bottom lip, mortified by her inane rambling. She never babbled. Usually, when matchmaking, she was tongue-tied. Her gaze darted away from his piercing blue eyes, and fixed on his mouth, which twitched, and then stretched into a grin.

Oh damn it! This was so not the way to talk to a client!

He stared at her mouth, and she fiddled with her glasses, breathing in a sigh of relief as Niall approached with a tray.

"Ah, here's Niall." He placed the drinks in front of them.

"Thanks."

Tiny beads of water frosted the outside of the glass. The stranger lifted it reverently and swallowed a long mouthful.

"I needed that." Teeth flashed white in his tanned face. "I haven't had a drink for weeks."

A likely story. He was enjoying the pint too much to be teetotal. He was even licking the foam off his top lip in a disturbingly sexy way.

"Sláinte." She raised her glass and drank deep,

ice clinking against her front teeth. Eventually, her scattered thoughts regrouped.

"My father's sick, so I'm taking over for the next few days."

"And that involves sitting in the pub?" He eyed her lazily, and swallowed more of his pint.

"Yes, I stay here until five o'clock." She opened the heavy black book, slipped her glasses back on, and uncapped her pen. "So, now, what's your name?"

"Jack Miller." She wrote it carefully on a pristine white page. "Is this necessary? I just need your father's help."

"I know. I can tell." Her cheeks heated in a blush. After five minutes she'd already managed to insult him.

"How exactly?" he asked slowly. "Are you psychic?"

Annie bit down on her tongue to stop from snapping back at him.

What was it her father had said? Male pride?

"You came into the bar looking for him, that's how. There's no mystery to it." She scanned him with a professional eye. He was a very good-looking man. Thick brown hair swept back from a tanned face with killer cheekbones most women would find attractive. She certainly did. His square chin was covered in dark stubble. He was a knockout. Or could be. If he made even the slightest attempt to make himself presentable.

She swallowed. *God, I hate this part of the job.*

"I'm not my father, but I'll be working closely with him. I know I can give you the help you need." She squared her shoulders pretending a bravery she didn't feel. "I need to find out a bit about you, and then I can help you."

"Right." He picked up the glass and drank. "What do you need to know?"

He leaned closer. Annie's heart thumped an irregular rhythm. Her mouth was suddenly parched, as though she'd been dragging herself through the desert. She pulled her bottom lip in, worrying it with her teeth. When his mouth stretched in a predatory grin, a shiver started somewhere in her solar plexus, moving inexorably downwards. Her response to him was ridiculous. She'd had men swarming around her all day. Her stupid body was reacting like she hadn't had any male attention in years.

Dad says men looking for love need encouragement. They need reassurance. God, he's good looking.

She swallowed.

"Well, I need to know what you're looking for in a woman." Annie fiddled with the corner of the book. She'd said the phrase a dozen times today already. This time was different. Embarrassment lit her face like an emergency beacon.

Jack grinned like a pirate, and then leaned back and crossed muscular forearms over his impressive chest. "I'm flattered, Honey." He covered her hand with his large brown one. "But I've just arrived. I'm hungry and tired after the trip, and I've things to take care of. You're gorgeous, but this'll have to wait." Her heart thudded in her chest.

Of all the arrogant...

Annie clenched her teeth and forced a tight smile. Surely, he didn't think she was coming on to him? Sharp fingernails cut into her palms. *I've got a job to do, and I promised Da I'd do my best. Throwing my drink at him isn't going to get me anywhere.*

"I need somewhere to stay. Can you recommend a hotel?"

She breathed in deeply. "You won't find a hotel, or a B and B. Not while the festival's on."

"Hold on a second, will you?"

He strode over to the bar while she drained her glass. All the time checking out his jean clad ass. Perfect. Some lady in the book was going to be very happy. She rubbed the lingering heat of his fingers from her hand, fighting off a contrary niggle of regret at the prospect of making a match for him.

In mere moments, he was back with a frown creasing his forehead.

"You're right. The barman says everything's

booked up." He swallowed the last inch of Guinness in his glass. "I need a few things for my boat, when's the Chandler's open?"

"Uncle Sean's closed for lunch, but he'll open up at two."

"Uncle Sean?" Black eyebrows rose.

"Yes." Discreetly Annie eased up the cuff of her jacket. One forty. "Whatever you need he'll have it, and if he doesn't he'll order it in." But she couldn't let him go yet. Da had told her what to do. Despite her disastrous morning, she had to try to make Jack Miller a match, no matter how uncomfortable it was talking to him about private stuff.

She squared her shoulders, and dived right in. "Jack, you sought me out for a reason. I know I'm not what you were expecting, but I would like you to give me a chance."

His eyes shuttered, and his mouth set in a stubborn line. He was as difficult to read as a book wrapped in cellophane.

"Devine's have been matchmakers of Durna for three generations." *And I sound like I'm narrating a documentary.* "We have a tried and tested method. First, we take a picture of you." Annie flicked back a couple of pages to show him. "Then, I interview you to find out what you're looking for in a partner."

Surprise flickered in Jack's eyes chased by a slow grin.

"Finally, with my father's help, I'll try and make you a match with one of the ladies in the book. You can meet, have a drink…" Annie's voice tapered off.

He shook his head firmly. "No," he said. "That's not going to happen."

Anger took over at the unfairness of it. Annie clenched her fists into tight balls. Bit her lip to resist the urge to shout at him.

I'm a complete washout, and it's only the first day. Her shoulders drooped in dejection. *I can't even persuade a complete stranger to take a chance and let me match him. It's not fair!*

Annie rose and stretched up to her full five foot two.

"Jack." She stood akimbo, hands on hips, like Julian in the Famous Five. A stance she hadn't resorted to since she was a kid, and wanted to look 'plucky and brave.'

I need a chance to turn this around. I'm going to have to beg for it. She sucked in a fortifying breath. *Here goes.*

"I understand you were expecting to meet my father here today, and might prefer to work with a man."

Jack was about to interrupt so she placed a hand on his arm to silence him. It was difficult enough, having to plead for his business, without his butting in all the time. His lazy smile vanished.

"My father is sick, and can't be here. He's entrusted me with his *vocation*," Annie stressed. "And even though I'd prefer to be in my flat in Dublin, I'm it, for the next thirteen days of the festival. My father needs me, and I'm determined to do my very best for everyone who comes seeking his services."

Jack glanced at her hand resting on his arm. She hurriedly removed it. "I'm just asking you to give me a chance."

"What's involved?" His eyes narrowed and her heart flipped over in delight.

She gestured toward the chair, and joined him when he sat down again. "Well, like I said, we start with a photo." Annie scanned his unkempt appearance with a studied eye. "Although, to be honest, if we're going to introduce you to a woman you should clean up a bit first to give you the best chance."

His faded jeans could do with a wash. It took a monumental effort of will to ignore the way his firm thighs filled them.

"It would be good if you had something a bit better to wear, too." He was quiet, too quiet. He was probably insulted. She softened her tone, and tried again. "We need to present you in your best possible light. There's a lot of competition during the matchmaking festival and the ladies can be very discerning you know."

"The matchmaking festival." Jack echoed slowly. "Right. And I've always had a problem attracting the ladies."

Annie reached out and patted his bicep. *Good. He'd taken her comments to heart. He was reaching out and being honest.*

"That's nothing to feel ashamed about, Jack." She lowered her voice and leaned closer. "Lots of men find meeting women intimidating or difficult, and that's why we're here. Just put yourself in my hands, and I'll set you up."

Did she really just tell him to put himself into her hands? Good Lord, why couldn't she talk to him without putting her foot in it? She crossed her fingers underneath the table. Maybe he was going to be a gentleman and not respond to her unintended double entendre. The corner of his mouth twitched, but he stayed mercifully silent.

Good. I've got away with it.

"Well, I need somewhere to stay…" Jack's eyebrows creased.

"I'll call the hotel and see if there are any last minute cancellations." Annie flipped open her mobile and scrolled through the numbers.

"Hi, I've someone here who needs a room, have you any cancellations?" The answer was negative. "Thanks anyway, Carly." Annie closed the phone. "Carly's parents own the only hotel in Durna and they're full."

She flipped the phone open again, talking rapidly to the person on the other end. Afterward she faced Jack. "Right, it's sorted. During the festival, everyone rents out a room or two in their house. There are so many people looking for somewhere to stay, we have to. My mother had a cancellation yesterday. You go and do what you need to do, Mr Miller, and then meet me back here. You're coming home with me."

A stunned expression flickered across his features. Then Jack nodded and sauntered out of the Maiden Arms. Heading out into a brightening sky, and the blue Atlantic Ocean.

THE SMELL of grilled steak in the air turned first Jack's nose, and then his whole body toward it. His stomach growled in anticipation of a non-tin based meal. Up the hill past a row of houses facing the sea was an Italian restaurant. His pace quickened.

"Table for one." He followed a young waiter to a table.

His hungry eyes scanned the menu.

Ah, this was more like it.

"Fillet steak, hold the pepper sauce, a double

order of sautéed potatoes, and a bottle of Chianti." The now calming sea was visible out of the large picture window.

What on earth have I got myself into? He'd spotted her the moment he walked into the bar. Couldn't believe his luck when the barman sent him her direction. She was really cute when she blushed. He grinned. She hadn't liked telling him he was good-looking either.

The waiter poured a small amount of wine. Jack lifted the glass to his lips, rolling the rich taste around in his mouth. "Perfect."

The waiter filled his glass.

"So, you're having a festival?"

"We have the matchmaking festival here every year." The young waiter seemed excited. *Maybe not much else happened in Durna.* "People come from everywhere for it. It's world famous."

"I think I just met the matchmaker." Jack lowered his voice to avoid being overheard. "Annie Devine?"

"Annie's father is the matchmaker, but she's taking over this year. He's not well so his wife isn't letting him out." The waiter pushed a hand over his buzz cut. "I think Annie was sort of thrown in at the deep end. She lives in Dublin now but came up yesterday to take his place."

"She married?" Jack held his breath. He couldn't remember when he was last intrigued by a woman, but there was something incredibly attractive about Annie Devine. It would be just his luck if she had a jealous husband tucked away somewhere.

"Annie's single. But I'm pretty sure she's not in the market for a boyfriend."

Jack blasted the young man with his most powerful glare. The waiter was talking as if he owned Annie.

The waiter fidgeted and glanced away. "I'm sorry. I was rude. We're all a bit over protective of Annie."

No kidding. "No harm done, I was only asking."

Annie was getting more interesting by the minute. Her long hair, unflattened by a hair straightener, tumbled in soft waves to just above her breasts. He didn't ever think he'd seen hair such a fascinating color. It was a mass of different shades; like the burnished walnut dash of the boat. Unlike most of the women he knew, she didn't plaster herself with make-up either. Her skin was clear and luminous, only lightly tanned, rather than fake baked. When she'd smiled, a dimple had teased in her cheek. He hadn't even known he loved dimples before then. Her eyes were the color of rich chocolate. When her gaze fixed on his he'd blazed to his shoes.

The waiter brought his steak. Jack closed his eyes and bit into the tender meat. The flavor rushed over his starved taste buds. If the restaurant were empty, he would have moaned aloud.

One thing at a time.

SURELY IT WAS *time to go home?*

Annie rubbed her throbbing forehead. In the past couple of hours, a sea of people had drifted to her table; her face ached from smiling. So many people looking for love, all of them terrified of rejection. Well, it made sense really. With her history, she couldn't blame them. Rejection sucked. And in such a close knit community it was a very public humiliation. She hated being the focus of gossip. The last thing she needed was a love affair, but Jack Miller was tempting her away from that point of view.

"Oh, thanks, Niall." Yet another cup of coffee. She would be buzzing all night.

"How's it going?" After a quick glance to make sure he had no customers waiting, Niall sat down.

"Not too well." Disappointment clawed at her insides. "I've done the interviews and taken their pictures, but they'd all be much happier talking to my father."

"I suppose they're used to talking to a man."
He patted her hand. "They'll come around."

An aging farmer paused mid-step when he
spied Annie in Bull's usual chair. Indecision
flickered and for a moment it looked like he was
going to run, but he clenched his jaw and kept
walking steadily towards her.

"Give it your best shot," Niall whispered.
"That's all you can do."

Half an hour later, Annie shook the balding
farmer's hand. *It's difficult to know who's more relieved
that's over.* Suddenly, the hairs on her nape stood
up, and her body hummed in awareness as a
familiar figure strode toward her.

"I'm back." Jack slid into the seat opposite.
"Are you still offering me a room, or am I going
back to the boat?"

"You're coming home with me. I told you; it's
all arranged." Annie closed the book and snagged
her jacket from the chair back. "I'm finished for
the day. Are you ready to go?"

"Yes. I've brought a few things from the boat. I
was hoping to find a launderette."

"You can use the washing machine and dryer
at home."

He followed her out.

"My car's over here."

Jack folded his long frame awkwardly into the

passenger seat. There was a scant inch above his head. He wasn't built for a Mini.

Potholes littered the road on the way to the little house facing the sea where she'd grown up. She bounced up and down on the hard seat as the Mini bounded over them. The suspension was so hard it was like being on a space-hopper built for two.

"Sorry about the potholes." She turned off the road and parked behind her parents' house. He was asleep. Sooty lashes brushed his cheeks. His hair stood up at the back as though stiff with salt. The magic paintbrush of sleep had erased the wrinkles around his eyes, making him look younger, more vulnerable somehow. *How can he affect me so strongly even when he's asleep?* Her libido ran riot imagining his firm lips teasing hers. Her core heated and her hand moved of its own volition to stroke his cheek.

"We're here." Her heart fluttered, caught in a sensuous spell. Electric-blue eyes opened slowly, their sleepy expression sharpening into instant desire. His gaze fell to her mouth.

Heat blazed as she pulled in a shaky breath. His shoulders were too close in the narrow seat. His thighs too close to hers. The heat was suddenly stifling.

She pulled her fingers away from his face, and gripped them in her lap. They tingled with the imprint of warm skin and whiskers. An electric current arced between them as he leaned closer. The air between their lips sizzled.

A door slammed loudly. Annie jerked away from the lure of Jack's warm mouth, eyes wide with shock.

"We're here," she croaked. "Come and meet my mother."

She jumped out of the car before he had a chance to react.

TWO

Jack rubbed gritty eyes with his fingers.

What the hell?

The small, dark haired seductress was hugging her mother so he stayed where he was. He scratched his jaw to banish the buzz of Annie's warm fingers on his face.

After a couple of minute's rapid-fire chat they turned and caught him staring. *Busted.* He untangled himself from the tiny car and plastered on a smile. Roxie was always telling him if he didn't, strangers were terrified of him.

"Mum, this is Jack."

Annie's chestnut gaze focused on his neck, avoiding his eyes. She flushed red. The girl was useless at hiding her emotions.

"Jack Miller." He proffered his hand.

"I'm Maeve," Annie's mother clutched it in an iron grip, and shook. "Welcome to our home, Jack. Come in." He followed her into the house's cool interior. "So, have you traveled up from Dublin?"

"No, I sailed in."

Her mouth stretched into a smile and her eyes sparkled. "Sailed? That's a new one. Were you traveling long?"

"I've been at sea for three weeks."

Annie looked astonished.

"I'm apologizing in advance. The shower broke in the boat and I'm not as fragrant as I could be!"

"I'll show you straight up to your room. You have your own bathroom with plenty of hot water, so that'll be soon sorted. Are you hungry? Can I fix you something to eat?"

"No thanks. I was fantasizing about steak, so I tracked one down the minute I got in."

Maeve grabbed fluffy towels from the airing cupboard, and eased open the door to a bedroom. A large double bed filled one wall, covered in a soft yellow quilt. It was clean and airy, with a fantastic view of the garden.

"This looks great." The smell of cut grass wafted in from the open window. In the distance, a blue swathe of sea sparkled in the sunlight.

"Your bathroom's over there."

Maeve glanced at the rucksack slung over his shoulder, and pulled open the wardrobe door. "And there's plenty of room to hang your things. I think you'll find everything you need, but if you don't just holler," she added before disappearing down the corridor.

Annie was quiet.

The hair stood up on the back of his neck. She was staring at him. He just knew it.

"You didn't tell me you were at sea for three weeks."

"You didn't ask." He kicked off his shoes at the foot of the bed and reached for the towels. "Now, if you'll excuse me…" Jack smothered a smile as she bristled, turned on her heels and disappeared after her mother.

In the bathroom, he grinned at the unfamiliar face in the mirror. *No wonder Annie thought I'd have to work hard to attract a mate!*

He pushed matted strands of hair back from his face, grimacing in pain as his scalp protested. Not his usual look, by any means. In fact, he was pretty sure none of his business colleagues would recognize this shabby stranger as the millionaire owner of Miller Advertising. None of their shoulders would be aching as his did either. The last struggle with the yacht in the storm was a lot more taxing than his weekly squash game. A long hot bath should help.

Steam billowed from the hot stream cascading into the deep enamel bath. A large glass bottle, stoppered with a cork, sat on the shelf, next to a cracked bar of soap. The thick liquid inside was a transparent gold, probably not lavender or rose then, he didn't want to smell like anyone's granny. Jack forced open the tight closure with finger and thumb to take a tentative sniff. Vanilla. Perfect. Subtle and not too sweet. A thin golden stream poured into the steaming torrent created a foaming mass of bubbles.

He stripped off his clothes, and climbed in.

The scent of vanilla filled the air as he rubbed bubbles over his chest and closed his eyes. He stretched his legs out in the hot water, edging down to see how much of himself he could fully submerge. It was the longest bathtub he'd ever been in, and his chest welled with satisfaction as the silky water covered him.

Annie Devine. She really was divine. She probably didn't even know how attractive she looked perched on the chair with the big book open in front of her. She wasn't his usual type. In fact, she was the complete antithesis of what Roxie called 'the blonde army' of his previous girlfriends.

"They're all the same, Jack. Tall, blonde, successful and confident. When are you going to give a real woman a chance?" Roxie had ranted more than once. The one thing about the blonde army was they understood the rules. His relationships followed carefully set guidelines. They were fun, they were exclusive, and they weren't permanent. Jack didn't need anyone, and he didn't want anyone to need him. Those types of complications only led to heartache. And he wasn't going there again.

Annie was a real woman. She was attracted to him, too. Even though she'd avoided holding his gaze too long, her small pink tongue had flicked out to moisten her lips when they met and she'd nervously fiddled with the ragged corner of the book.

She'd stood out like a beacon in the mustiness of the bar. Her long sleeved blue cotton shirt perfectly showcased her breasts. When she'd walked out of the pub in front of him he'd got a great view of long legs and a small but curvy behind inside tight jeans. He skimmed a hand through the acres of bubbles and sank under the water.

The Chandler, Sean Devine said it would take days to get the boat ready to sail to Dun Laoghaire. He would be stuck here for a week at least, right in Annie's house. Maybe playing lovesick bachelor would be an amusing diversion.

He squeezed out a nut of shampoo and massaged it into his hair. *She was so insistent I give her a try I had to surrender.* Deceit niggled, but he shrugged it off. If he got in too deep, he'd let her know what he was really doing in Ireland. Although frankly, that wasn't anybody's business but his.

THE BATHROOM DOOR creaked so loudly they heard it in the kitchen.

"He's a fine one." Maeve was digging for information, as usual.

"He's a client, Mum. Not a potential boyfriend." He was a fine one, there wasn't any denying it, but Annie'd rather walk over flaming coals than admit it. With both parents so skilled at the art of squeezing information out of people, changing the subject was always the best form of defense.

"How's Da?"

"Unbearable. He can't stand being out of the action." Maeve poured tea into mugs. "He's dozing out in the garden, waiting for you to be finished for the day. Take him out a cup will you, Love?"

Annie slipped the heavy matchmaking book under her arm. She grasped two mugs and slipped sideways through the back door her mother held open. A soft breeze teased her long strands of hair, lifting them. The air was redolent with the scent of summer. After a day stuck in the pub, the smell of freshly mown grass was the perfect antidote to warm beer, sour breath, and unwashed men.

Bull Devine sat on the rough-hewn chair his father had made under the spreading apple tree.

"I've brought us some tea, Da." Bull was already looking better. When he took to his bed last week they were all worried. He hadn't visited the doctor for years because he hadn't needed to, and always refused to go for a check-up. This time he was so sick he hadn't even had the strength to complain when the doctor arrived at his bedside.

"It's just a chest infection, Annie." Maeve confided on the phone after the doctor prescribed antibiotics and left. "Thank God."

She passed over the tea, and settled down next to him.

There was a movement in the window upstairs. Through the lacy veil of blossoms, there was a sudden glimpse of naked male torso.

If she were alone, she would have sat and stared. But she wasn't, so averted her gaze quickly. It didn't help. The mental image of a wet, naked Jack burned into her retina. Her temperature raised by a couple of degrees, and she fanned her face with her hand, to cool down. She gulped a mouthful of tea, moistening her suddenly dry mouth.

"Hi, Annie. Tough day?" Bull's words brought her back down to earth with a bump.

"The worst. God only knows how you manage it, year after year. I'm wrecked."

She stretched out her legs and slipped her shoes off, wriggling her toes in the damp grass. "I didn't do very well, I'm afraid." The breeze whipped her hair into her eyes. "I had trouble with some of the local guys. The older ones were quiet and embarrassed. And the younger ones that I was in school with, flirted relentlessly. I've spent years dodging the attentions of many of them, and there I was, asking them what they were looking for in a woman."

Annie grimaced. The day had been like a bad reality show with her as one of the hapless contestants. Maybe if she treated information gathering as a series of challenges to be overcome it would be easier.

"When Liam Mackey told me I was exactly what he was looking for, I nearly slapped him." Why on earth Liam Mackey thought for a moment she'd be interested when he'd stuffed frogs in the pocket of her painting smock when they were seven, and splashed her riding his bike through a puddle when they were nine...

"They're nervous, Annie." Bull's puppy dog

eyes dissolved her irritation. The man was really good at what he did. Master manipulators made the best matchmakers. "Men want love in their lives, but they're frightened of rejection, I've told you that."

He had. Repeatedly. In fact, it was Bull's favorite lecture. *The vulnerability of the mate- seeking male.*

"I can't help thinking if I was married, or at least involved with someone it'd be different." Annie frowned. When she was with Steve, she hadn't had this problem. But then again, she hadn't been asking the locals what they were looking for in a woman. "As it is, they seem to think I'm interviewing for a boyfriend."

"They all know you're single. And I guess there's always the possibility you might indeed be looking for a boyfriend." He held his hands up in surrender as her mouth opened to protest. "I know you're not, but they don't. Even if they're not applying for the position, the opportunity to practice chat up lines on a captive female is probably too good to resist."

Bull's face screwed up like a tissue. "Sorry, Love. I haven't much to suggest. I don't have the same problem when I'm matchmaking." His shoulders lifted and fell in defeat.

"You should have made me a match, Da. I've asked you often enough," Annie teased.

"I've never met the one for you, Annie. I'll let you know when I do though."

"Yes, and the next time you warn me off someone I'll listen. It was such a fiasco." She picked an apple blossom off the tree above them, twirling the flower around between her fingers. Her one foray into love had been an unmitigated disaster. *Who needs it?* She threw the bloom to the grass, discarding unpleasant memories with the flower.

"Will I open it up and tell you what I've got?" He'd been sneaking glances at the book, as if dying to see if there was anyone new, who might be the ideal match for one of his clients. Matchmaking wasn't just something her clever father did during the annual festival. His thoughts turned to love twenty-four hours a day, seven days a week.

For years, Annie avoided bringing home a boyfriend, or a male friend of any type. Living up to his nickname, Bull went for the direct approach. When she was eighteen, Mick Ryan had taken her to the prom. Upstairs, getting ready, she'd heard Bull grill him on the doorstep, before reluctantly admitting him. Reeling from the third degree, Mick had relaxed when he met her mother. *Bad mistake.* Her expert interrogation gleaned a hell of a lot more than his name, rank and serial number.

After Mick, she'd introduced them to her fiancé, Steve. They hadn't liked him, even before her disastrous wedding day. As she slid into her wedding dress, Steve got into the ten o'clock train to Dublin with Elaine Sweeney. The news spread like wildfire before the train even pulled out from the station. He hadn't even had the decency to leave a note. With one fell swoop she'd gone from bride to jilted. Her parents went into complete and utter shock. The bridesmaid was no help, she hadn't turned up that morning, too busy getting ready for her train journey. Without a sibling to take over, she'd had no option but to stifle her mortification and stalk into the church in full wedding dress, to tell the congregation the wedding was off. Afterward, she regretted not wearing the veil.

Thank goodness I now have my own home. Her small flat in Dublin was miles away from the scene of the crime. A bolthole where she could be herself. Could live her own life.

Annie's heart ached at the remembered betrayal. Elaine had been her friend since they were kids, and Steve… She forced the feeling down and opened the book.

JACK STRIPPED the packaging from the mobile broadband stick bought in Durna's only technology shop, and plugged it into his laptop. He connected his headphones and mike, and dialed New York.

"Roxie? It's Jack."

"Jack!" Roxie started in to a lengthy, breathless questionfest. Not stopping to hear his answers. His eyes rolled at her excited flow of words. It was amazing how much his secretary talked. Even more amazing was the fact Jack found her constant chatter soothing. His mother had talked mile-a-minute too. There was a technique to talking with Roxie. Let her get it all out, and when she runs out of things to say, *strike*. She finally paused to draw breath.

"The yacht got struck by lightning."

She squeaked something girly. The words escaped him, but the tone was one of concern.

"I'm fine. I pulled in at a small village in the west of Ireland. I have to make some repairs to the boat before I continue to Dun Laoghaire."

"How was the journey—worth it?"

"Yes, definitely. I've learnt a lot about the yacht on the voyage. It'll make the presentation much weightier. I want you to do a couple of things for me."

"Okay, shoot." Roxie switched to efficiency mode.

"Confirm Monday's meeting with Bateau Rouge in Dublin. Have you organized my hotel?"

"Yes, Boss. You're booked into the Shelbourne for Sunday and Monday nights. I'll get the car transferred from Dun Laoghaire, they have a branch in Galway." The rapid clicking of keys showed she was right on it.

"Right, give me their number and I'll handle the pick up from here." Jack found an old envelope in his jacket pocket, and jotted down the name and telephone number.

"That's great, Roxie. Can you patch me though to Mark?" He gazed out of the window into the verdant green of the garden, so different from his usual view of grey waves, and greyer sky. A cloud of pink blossoms shrouded a large tree. Something moved under it.

"Jack, you made it!" The congratulatory tones of his second in command, Mark Windsor came onto the line.

"Hi Mark. Yes. It was a long and rough trip but I'm finally here."

"I'm staying put for the next few days. I'm in a town called Durna, it's on the west coast. I'm compiling the data from the sail for a presentation that should rock Bateau Rouge on Monday. How's everything with you? Have you presented to Mecredi Cars?"

"We're ready to go. The presentation's in a few hours." Mark sounded confident.

Jason Mecredi, owner and Chairman of Mecredi Cars, was notoriously difficult but Mark was ready to go solo on a presentation. He was perfect partner material, and it would be good to split the load.

"All right, Mark. I'll talk to you later. Give 'em hell." He hung up. Annie's voice drifted up to his window. She wasn't alone. He heard the deeper tones of a man.

She laughed warmly and his stomach clenched in an irrational burst of temper.

I guess the waiter's wrong. She's got a boyfriend after all. Acid burned in his gut. He turned away from the half-hidden cozy tableau beneath him to stuff his arms into a worn denim shirt. If she has a boyfriend, that's her business. He hadn't come to Ireland to flirt with a woman. He had a job to do. And a relative to find.

There were footsteps on the path below, then the heavy thud of the kitchen door. He rooted out his plastic bag of washing from the bottom of the knapsack and went downstairs.

The buzz of conversation ceased abruptly as he entered the kitchen.

"You clean up well." Maeve flicked the kettle on. "We'll be having dinner in a while; I hope you'll join us."

His stomach was full of steak. But he could force something else in. "That would be great, Mrs. Devine. I've no plans."

"Maeve." She spotted the bag hanging from his hand. "Washing?"

"Annie said…"

"I know, she told me." Maeve turned to her daughter. "Annie, take Jack out to the shed and introduce him to the washing machine. You'll find everything you need out there, Jack."

It was warm in the back garden. Annie silently walked around the corner to a small shed. The door squeaked open, and she stood back to let him pass.

He stopped.

"What's the matter?" She was so close every tiny eyelash was visible. The dark pool of her irises expanded, swallowing up the brown. Despite his determination not to get involved, he leant forward and breathed in deeply. A scent of flowers, and something lemony hung in the air.

Tangible waves of disquiet rolled off her. She ran the tip of her tongue over full, pink lips. Desire flashed instantly, like oxygen flowing onto sparks. How would she taste? She turned away, but he caught her by her upper arms and stepped into her personal space.

"Are you avoiding me?"

"No." She stepped back. "I'm just tired, that's all."

His hand moved to her jawline. "That's not all. There's something different about you." Her skin was warm, strokeably soft. He shouldn't be touching, but he couldn't resist. "I heard you laughing with a man, while I was getting dressed earlier. Will he be joining us for dinner?" Damn it, he sounded like a jealous lover. Sure, she'd leaned close to him in the car, let her fingers trail over his face, then gazed at him with big brown eyes as though she wanted to kiss him, but maybe it didn't mean anything. Maybe she got a kick from leading a guy on.

He rubbed his thumb slowly over her jawbone. She was attracted to him all right; her swift intake of breath was a dead giveaway. She swayed into his hand and her eyes drifted closed like a virgin sacrifice, offering herself. His traitorous body tightened in response. Some poor sap was going to be devastated if he took what she was so blatantly offering. He gulped and took a step away. Jack wouldn't be responsible for another man's heartbreak. He knew what that was like, and had vowed never to trust a woman again. He loved women. Their smell, their taste, the sound of their laughter. The last woman he'd given his heart to in New York had seemed devoted to him. Right up to the moment he caught her in bed with

someone else. He lived life by different rules now.
There were plenty of women who were interested
in spending time in his bed without falling in love.

"What?" Annie whispered.

"I said, will the man you were laughing with
earlier be joining us for dinner tonight?"

"Yes, he will." She chewed on her lip. "And we
better hurry up putting your clothes in the washer.
You look so much better since your bath. I'd like
to get a photo before the light goes."

She really was a piece of work.

"For the book," she spelled out calmly. "*I* don't
need a picture."

"Not while you have the real thing in front of
you anyway." He followed her into the shed; eyes
glued to the subtle sway of her hips.

"There's powder there. Set the washing
machine to four for a general wash."

"Right, I'll see you back at the house."

"I'll get my camera." She squeezed past him,
brushing against his skin. A tingle of electricity
shot up his arm, like the one that fried his boat
and forced him to pull in to Durna in the first
place. He frowned at her departing back. A raw
flash of lust was roaring to life at the mere
sensation of her flesh touching his. What would
full on skin-to-skin contact be like? He harshly
stuffed his clothes into the washing machine,
stunned by his body's reaction. Annie Devine was

dangerous. The last thing he wanted to do was have a fling with another woman he couldn't respect in the morning.

ANNIE TREMBLED. She jerked open the car door to grab her camera. She'd never been so confused in her entire life. One minute Jack was stroking her face, and the next looking at her with disgust in his eyes.

And her reaction to him…what was that about? She shivered. His body heat had scorched her in the doorway of the shed. She could have sworn she'd caught the faint scent of vanilla. Something was happening between them. Something she didn't want, and couldn't have. He was a sailor, for goodness sake. A man who spent long weeks at sea.

She hung the camera's strap around her neck. She had a life in the city, and her lifelong dream was so close she could taste it. A dream that would take her far away from the sea. Yet here she was, captivated by a sailor. When he touched her, she'd yearned for his mouth to grind down on hers. It was crazy. *He's a client. The one ironclad rule of matchmaking is not to poach the clients.*

Jack strode out of the shed toward the back door.

"Hold up, I'll take a picture of you now." He paused mid-step, and waited for her to catch up. Annie pointed the camera at him but he was so tall the result was a far from flattering shot up his nostril. She grinned. It wouldn't get him any dates. She half wanted to put it in the book anyway. To keep the women of Durna off him.

"You'll have to sit down."

She gestured at the cast iron chair and table her mother had placed at the back door.

"Right." Jack sat and scowled at her.

"Smile." He wasn't co-operating. If anything, his scowl darkened. "Oh come on, Jack, you can do better than that," she teased. "Remember you want women to look at this picture and choose you, rather than any of the other men in the book."

His eyes glinted a warning, but it was too late to take back the flirtatious words.

"What would make you choose me, rather than any of your other suitors?" A devastating grin transformed his face. She burned under its heat like a chicken on a spit.

"That'd do it," she muttered under her breath. "That'll do," she repeated loudly, snapping the shutter. "Let's go in for dinner."

He opened the door wide and stood back to let her stride into the kitchen before him.

THREE

Four places were set at the heavy pine table. As Jack waited for the final chair to be filled, his body tensed at the thought of meeting the sucker Annie was stringing along. The door creaked open. A heavyset man with graying hair shuffled arthritically to the table.

"I'm Brendan Devine." The newcomer held out his hand to Jack in welcome. "But everyone calls me Bull. You must be Jack." He pumped Jack's captured hand vigorously. "You're welcome to our house."

"Thank you." So this was the stranger. Not some boyfriend. He'd got it totally wrong. What was worse, Annie knew it. He ran his hand though his hair. "I think I heard you in the garden earlier."

"That would be right. I was getting a progress report from Annie. I can't stand not being in the thick of things with the festival being on, but the doctor's a tyrant." He leant closer, lowering his voice conspiratorially. "I've known him since he was a pup. I introduced his parents, but that doesn't get me any respect apparently. I have to take it easy until my chest improves. Maeve here has me more or less confined to bed. Normally I wouldn't mind it too much, but with the festival being on…"

"Potatoes, Da?"

Bull helped himself from the bowl Annie held.

"So that's why Annie is up in the pub, on the matchmaker's chair." Jack said.

"She's the next matchmaker. Or will be when I finally give it up."

Jack glanced at Annie. Surely, her family could see the look of dread flickering over her expressive face?

"That won't be for years, Da." She surreptitiously crossed the fingers of her right hand, and ate with her left.

"Tell us about yourself, Jack." Maeve's clear green gaze fastened to his like the guidance system of a heat-seeking missile.

"I've just sailed the Atlantic."

Annie gasped.

"And you came all this way for the festival?"

Maeve's eyebrows shot toward her hairline. Annie was going to be mad, but now was the time to come clean. Jack began to understand what people meant when they wished for the floor to open up and swallow them as three pairs of eyes swiveled his direction. He sipped some water to clear the tightness in his throat. *Here goes.* He put his fork down, clenching his napkin under the table and turned to Annie's steady chestnut gaze.

"No I didn't." Her eyes widened, and her rosebud mouth gaped. "Unfortunately Annie misunderstood."

"You came into the Maiden's Arms and asked for Devine," Annie interrupted. "I heard you."

"My yacht got struck by lightning. I had to make an emergency stop. When I came ashore, I saw the sign for the Chandlers. It was closed and I was directed to the pub. That's why…"

"That's why you were looking for Devine. You wanted Uncle Sean." She glared across the table. "You could have just told me. Not let me go on about how you were a good looking man, and all." A reddening flush swept her features and her fingers clenched into fists.

"I did try and tell you matching me was never going to happen."

She wasn't going to forgive him. Her jaw was set in a stubborn line.

"Ah well, no harm done," Maeve said briskly.

"Eat up now before it gets cold." The only coldness was the glacial draft blowing his direction from across the table. "Sean tells me you've fried everything, right enough. He says you won't be moving on for a few days yet."

He stared at Maeve in surprise. Annie's mother had obviously done her research, and knew his stay in Durna was more impulsive than planned.

"So, Bull. Did Annie find you any good prospects for the book?" Maeve winked at him. He puffed out a breath as the tension left his body.

"She got a good few, okay, although we'll have to take Jack out." Bull shoveled in another mouthful. "But she's having problems with some of the men."

"Ah, the old ones. They're used to talking to a man." Maeve said.

"The young ones too, Mum." Annie replied. "I've heard chat up lines today you wouldn't believe."

"Do you come here often?"

Her lips softened into a smile at his comment. A wave of relief flooded him as the tension between them eased.

"I heard it a couple of times, along with 'Heaven must be missing an angel...'"

"Because you're here with me, right now." Their eyes met and her soft lips parted slightly. If she responded like that every time, he couldn't blame them.

"The problem is they know you're single," Bull said. "That makes you easy game, especially if you're the matchmaker."

"Maybe I'll have better luck tomorrow." She stood up from the table and collected the plates.

"Now. Chocolate time?"

"Absolutely." Maeve cut some thin slices from an apple, and placed them on a plate. She passed it to Bull who slipped a slice into his mouth and chewed vigorously.

"It cleans your palate." He grinned at Jack. "We take chocolate tasting very seriously in this house."

Annie was decanting chocolates from a box on the counter onto small china plates. She placed one in front of each of them.

"Annie's brought these for us from Dublin, Jack. It's a sort of special treat." The abrupt change of subject was bewildering. What on earth was going on?

Annie smiled, taking obvious pleasure at his confusion. "Right, we are tasting two different types this evening. Elderflower Ganache and Almond Praline Truffle. You've two of each. Shall we start with the Elderflower?"

Bull picked up a chocolate and held it up. "It looks great, good and shiny."

Maeve agreed.

Jack picked up a chocolate and followed their lead. He'd heard of chocolate appreciation but these guys were crazy. They were taking it way too seriously.

"Now feel." Maeve rubbed her thumb gently over it. "Lovely. Smooth and silky."

All the comments seemed to be directed at Annie. *Bizarre.* He obediently felt the chocolate's smooth surface under his fingers.

"Can I taste it now?"

"No. Not yet." She shook her head, looking serious. "First you have to smell it."

Jack stifled a grin as Maeve and Bull closed their eyes and sniffed the chocolates. This was really getting ridiculous.

"Smell it, Jack." Annie frowned, and to keep the peace he brought the chocolate to his nose and gave it a cursory sniff.

"Great." He had no idea what he was supposed to be doing. This sure wasn't the way he ate chocolates. His usual technique consisted of stuff it in, chew and swallow.

"Now, we can taste." Annie held up a finger in warning. "But don't just toss it in there and chew, Jack. You need to put the chocolate into your mouth and wait for it to melt."

"Umm, the melting point." Maeve carefully

placed the chocolate in her mouth and waited, as if expecting an alarm clock to start ringing.

"Okay, go ahead."

The heady taste of chocolate bloomed on his tongue. He pressed the candy to the roof of his mouth. Delicious. The soft, creamy center dissolved, and an intense flowery flavor teased his taste buds. His eyes closed and he surrendered to the full sensual onslaught of the chocolate. *So that's why women love it so much.* When he reluctantly opened them, Annie was staring at him, her pupils huge.

"That has got to be the best chocolate I've ever tasted." He licked the remnants from his top lip. Her eyes flickered to his mouth, setting off an uncomfortable tightening in his body.

"Thank you."

Was she aware of his body's reaction to her? Jack shifted in his seat. It wasn't the time or the place to be having a private moment with her parents sitting right there with them. He glanced sideways. Bull was popping his second chocolate into his mouth with a look of pure bliss on his face. Good, nobody seemed to have noticed.

"Annie, you've outdone yourself," Maeve said.

Realization dawned. "You made these?"

Annie nodded, and straightened the plate with nervous fingers. "I'm a chocolatier. These are my entries for the Chocolate Oscars competition. The elderflower ganache got me through to the semi-finals."

"I'm not surprised, they're wonderful." The contents of his plate looked as good as they tasted. "Do you make them here?"

"I used to, when I was learning. Now I make them in my flat in Dublin." Her shy smile was enchanting. "I have all my equipment and supplies there. It takes up quite a lot of space."

"They're delicious, Darling." Maeve recovered from her chocolate induced trance. "What's the other one?"

"It's a praline. A different type of chocolate to demonstrate my range." She picked one up and looked at it. "This is my semi-final entry. Everybody ready to try one?"

This time Jack knew what was coming. The bizarre ritual grew on him and he looked, felt and smelled the chocolate with the others. His mouth watered as the heady aroma stimulated his senses.

Annie placed one into her mouth, her small pink tongue visible as her lips parted to receive it. *God, who knew chocolate tasting could be so goddamned erotic?*

He couldn't look away. The moment her chocolate started to melt a look of ecstasy came over her face. Her eyelids fluttered shut and a half smile of total bliss smoothed her features. *What would it be like to kiss her now?*

He followed her lead. As it melted, he bit in to the dissolving chocolate. The texture of finely ground nuts slightly abrasive against his over-sensitized tongue. He moaned, swirling the thick filling over his tongue. She was a genius. The flavors were so perfectly matched the immediate rush of the chocolate blended with the praline perfectly, fading to a warm cocoa aftertaste.

"God, those are good."

"I delivered a batch of these to the judges in Dublin before I came up yesterday. If I win, I'm through to the finals. Then I'll have to produce my top chocolate."

"Which is?"

She was dangerously fascinating, and fast becoming irresistible. "Divine. I just call it Divine."

"Did you bring one for us to taste?" The white cardboard box on the counter was too far away to check.

"No, Divine is under wraps."

"Until they ask for it," he finished. She didn't need to explain, he knew why.

There was a magical purity about creation. The moment before revealing your greatest creation was one to be guarded jealously; lest any of the magic should dissipate. It was the same in his business. Jack let his ideas for an advertising campaign take careful form. Allowing them to develop, like all the subtle flavors in one of Annie's creations, before presenting to a client. Once the client had seen the campaign, the moment was broken. Up until then, the magic needed to be kept safe. He and Annie Devine had more in common than he'd thought.

"I'll put the kettle on." Maeve walked to the counter. "Annie, take Jack out to put his things in the dryer, he'll get lost in the dark."

ANNIE GLANCED out at the darkening sky. *He can see perfectly well, but Mum will be appalled if I refuse.* She battled with conflicting emotions at the thought of being outside in the dark with Jack Miller. The revelation he was a transatlantic sailor had been a shock. When she'd found out he wasn't a client, and remembered all the things she'd said to him, her embarrassment had turned fairly quickly into anger.

Despite herself, his reaction to her chocolates had dissolved her anger at his deception. His face had changed when he bit into the first chocolate. *Would he look like that if they were making love?* Rough waves of desire flooded her. By the time he'd touched the second chocolate to his lips she was so turned on she thought she might combust. It was only the presence of her parents in the kitchen that stopped her from walking up and licking the trace of chocolate off those firm molded lips.

He's dangerous. She walked to the back door. *And he's not a client any more, so he's available.* She stepped out onto the rough cement path on the way to the shed.

"You're supposed to be making sure I don't fall in the dark." His warm hand grasped hers in the darkness. "Not run away from me."

"I'm not running anywhere." She faced him. "Although after today I think I'd be entitled. Don't you have anything to say to me?"

"I told you matchmaking me wasn't going to happen," he replied stubbornly. "And you begged me to give you a chance."

"So you do want to meet a woman then." She tried to pull her hand away.

"I don't." He gripped her hand tightly. The rough ridges of his thumb stroked the sensitive skin on the back of her hand, playing havoc. "In fact, before you touched me, the last thing I wanted to do was meet a woman." His voice was so low it was only a grumble in the darkness.

She'd touched first. *Trust him to remember.*

"Huh." She tugged her hand out of his grip. "You'll have to do better if you think I'm going to forgive the dance you led me. You even sat out here this evening and let me take your picture.

Why did you do that if you've no intention of going in the book?"

She reached the door and flicked on the light.

"I have trouble saying no to you." He walked past her and pulled his clothes out of the washing machine. "I have a feeling it's a common complaint around here." He stuffed the wet clothes into the drier. She ignored him. It was too tempting to forgive and surrender to his flirtations, but a trace of humiliation lingered. She wasn't inclined to let him off the hook so easily.

"You misled me. You weren't honest," she insisted stubbornly, scrutinizing his butt as he bent to place the last handful of clothes in the dryer.

"Like you're honest." He straightened and caught her staring.

"Yes." She crossed her hands in front of her chest. The thin cotton shirt wasn't doing a very good job at hiding her erect nipples.

"But you're not honest."

"What do you mean I'm not honest? I am!" It was as though she had signs pointing all her buttons out in neon, and he was pressing them.

"Then why don't you tell them you dread the idea of being the next matchmaker?"

The color drained from her face. *How had he worked it out?*

"I don't know what you're talking about."

"I thought you were honest?" he challenged,

gripping her upper arms. "I saw your face when your father told me, Annie. Don't try and fool me."

"I'm not trying to fool anyone." Being the matchmaker was more than a job. It was her destiny. Her dreaded inheritance. "I just don't know how to tell him."

The touch of his hands set off an unwanted blaze of reaction. She scooted away, and his hands dropped to his sides. She rubbed her upper arms vigorously banishing the disturbing tingle that overcame her body every time Jack touched her.

"So, now you know how I felt," he answered, wryly. "But at least I came clean. You need to tell them. They'll understand."

"No. They won't."

She'd struggled with the idea of telling them for years. Finally, she'd avoided the problem by leaving. With Durna out of sight, it had been blissfully out of mind. But a problem avoided wasn't a problem solved. Being back for the festival had brought it dead center again.

"There's always been a Devine matchmaker at the festival. My father expects me to continue the tradition. If I had any brothers or sisters perhaps I'd have a chance, but I don't..." *How could she explain her feelings to him? She couldn't even deal with them herself.*

"I don't know what I'm going to do about it,

which is why I haven't told anyone how I feel." It was something she'd wrestled with forever. The most difficult challenge she'd faced since Steve left her at the altar. She didn't want to disappoint her father. He'd be crushed. "You have to promise not to talk about it. It's going to be hard to tell them. I'll have to cross that bridge when I come to it."

"So you're just going to pretend?"

"Right now, yes." She willed him to understand.

"I don't get it. You're an adult, Annie. You control your own life; you shouldn't live it by anyone else's rules." He turned to face her, and placed his hands on his hips.

"I want to open a shop in Dublin. And you don't know me or my family. I can't break my father's heart by telling him I don't want to be the next matchmaker. It's not that easy." She brushed the hair tumbling into her eyes away. Challenged him with her glare. "Do you do everything you want?"

"Yes." Jack stepped closer and ran his thumb over her bottom lip. His eyes darkened to stormy blue. "I do."

He wanted to kiss her. She felt it in the powerful electricity that surged through her at the touch of his calloused thumb against her mouth. Her heart hammered in her chest as warring emotions battled within her. Give in to desire, or get away before she did something she might regret. She took the easy option.

"It's cold out here. Let's go back in." She swiveled on her heel and hurried down the path, every molecule stretched tight with awareness of his presence, following.

FOUR

Annie dragged the duvet up to her ears and curled her legs closer to her body. Outside the window, tree branches swayed from side to side in the darkness and bats swooped fast and low, hunting moths attracted to the faint light cast by the rooms below.

Drawn to the light just like I'm drawn to Jack. Everything came back to the man lying in the bed in the next room. Even now, with a busy day of matchmaking ahead, her ears strained for any sound through the thick walls.

Her long ago attraction to Steve was water compared to the whiskey kick of excitement that flooded her senses when Jack's thumb had caressed her mouth. It threw her off kilter. Too tongue tied to make casual conversation after the incident in the laundry room, she'd escaped early to bed.

The bed was as lumpy as ever. She relieved some tension by pounding her pillows, and then rearranged them and tried to settle again. It was no use. Her hormones were in an uproar. Her imagination running overtime.

I know what I want from life, and Jack Miller isn't it.

She closed her eyes tight, willing herself to sleep.

Liar.

THE SEA GLISTENED in the midday sun. Diamond flickers of light bounced off the tiny caps of the waves. An off-sea breeze plastered Jack's tee shirt to his chest and he angled his right shoulder forward to deflect it. His calves burning at the unaccustomed exercise, he stopped for a moment to stretch out his straining muscles. He pushed his toes skyward in a hamstring stretch, and continued down the road again. Last night had been a disaster, one he was determined to mitigate. It would take time to repair the boat. Hopefully his relationship with Annie could be repaired more quickly.

The lunchtime crowd teemed around the pub like wasps around an apple tree. Jack eased his way through them into the dark interior. It took a moment to adjust after the sun's brightness. Annie held court at the matchmaker's table.

If the pub was an apple tree, Annie was a pot full of jam, totally surrounded by buzzing men. Or a lighthouse, standing steady in a testosterone sea, which ebbed and flowed around her. She wasn't flirting. The short denim skirt and long black leather boots encasing her long, shapely legs were doing that for her. Her tee-shirt couldn't be any closer to her chest if it were sprayed on.

She flicked her mane of chestnut hair over her shoulder. It tumbled down her back like a sinuous ribbon.

A soft silky …

He clenched his fists tightly. *Get a grip.*

A figure stepped out of the swarm, moving close enough to touch. Blood rushed to his head and his feet ate up the distance between them, but not quickly enough. The young buck reached out and stroked a lazy finger down her arm.

"Will you come for lunch with me, Annie?" the teenager asked.

She turned to the boy and gently removed his hand with a soft smile.

"Sorry, Michael…"

Jack clenched his fists at his sides, and plastered on a smile.

"Hi, Darling. Sorry I'm late."

Her mouth opened and closed like a stunned goldfish. Her long eyelashes blinked, and her chestnut eyes gazed into his. A lone eyelash escaped in the movement and he stroked it away. His breath caught in his throat when the color of her eyes intensified to chocolate at his touch.

"Jack." He captured the small hand Annie pushed against his chest. Like the opening step of a dance, Jack's hand curled around her ribcage and propelled her closer. Blood pounded in his ears as his lips met hers. She sighed, and her hand slid up around his neck.

The buzz of conversation faded and time stopped. Her tongue touched his and he deepened the kiss. Her fingers stroked his neck, slid into his scalp. Someone coughed, breaking the spell and thrusting the reality of the situation front and centre. Dazed, he opened his eyes. This wasn't the time. It certainly wasn't the place.

He drew back, holding on to her elbow.

"I've booked us a table in Mario's." He made a pretense of studying his Rolex.

"We better go."

She stretched across the table for her handbag and the matchmaking book. A pack of male eyes tracked her movement.

Jack smiled at the unfamiliar faces. "I'm Jack Miller." He stuck his hand out to Annie's disappointed suitor who could barely make eye contact as he shook it.

Before she could protest, Jack grabbed Annie's hand, and wove through the crowd to the door. He strode up the hill towards the restaurant while she trotted beside him trying to keep up.

SHE SHOULD HAVE WORN SOCKS. The back of her heels burned against the black leather. She puffed out a breath and clenched her teeth. There would be a showdown, but they could do without an audience. An opportunity arose as they drew parallel to a small laneway and she shoved him sideways into it. He stumbled. Stopped.

"Annie! What the hell?" She grabbed him by his upper arms and slammed him back against the worn brickwork of the building.

"What did you think you were doing?" The potent buzz of anger infused every pore. "What sort of idiot caveman are you?"

He'd kissed her. In front of everyone. She scrunched her eyes tight shut to blot out the memory. And, stupidly, she'd let him. With a snort of disgust, she dropped her hands to her sides and moved away. He'd better have a good excuse for kissing her, because she didn't have a clue why she'd kissed him back.

"You needed my help." Jack clenched his jaw and crossed his arms over his chest. "They were all over you in there."

A tension headache stabbed between her eyes. *Oh great. Hero complex.*

"I did *not* need your help. I can take care of myself; I've been doing it for years. The last thing I needed was you pawing me in front of the whole town. You've made a show of me." She bit her lip, the repercussions of her very public response to him fully sinking in. Her privacy was the most important thing to her. And she'd just tossed it away by kissing him.

"They all already think I'm desperate. Now every guy in the village will think I'm easy too. I'll be fighting them off with a stick," she muttered wryly. This was morphing into the weekend from hell. Before she melted back to Dublin, the grapevine would be buzzing with more news on her love life. Just what she *didn't* need.

He shoved away from the wall towards her. She glared, effectively halting his approach. "I kissed you for a reason, and it wasn't the obvious one."

"So you didn't want to, then?" The words escaped before she could restrain them. Why should she care whether he wanted to kiss her or not? She didn't want him to. That was all there was to it.

"Yes, I bloody wanted to." His brows furrowed, and his mouth flattened into a thin line. "But that's not why I did it. You had Michael feeling you up…"

"He touched my arm!" she shouted. "In what, twisted parallel universe are you living, when a guy I've known all my life touching my arm qualifies as feeling me up?"

She stalked away, resisting the urge to kick over a pile of old cardboard boxes stacked against the wall. A scrawny cat glanced their direction, and then sniffed hungrily at a half eaten hamburger lying in a discarded fast food container.

God, he was a complete Neanderthal. Not in any way worthy of the hours spent fantasizing about him last night. He was *way* out of order.

She sucked in a lungful of sea damp air. Their kiss was going to be the talk of the village by the time they'd finished lunch. They needed damage limitation, and fast.

"Right, Jack." Like a dog worrying a bone, she couldn't let it be. "Enlighten me. Why the kiss?"

"You liked it then?" His grin transformed his thundercloud expression as if the sun had suddenly come out. He gazed into her eyes. Her lips tingled as anger evaporated, replaced by a heavy tension. It charged the air between them like the split second before a lightning strike.

"Whether I liked it or not is totally beside the point." She spelled it out. Slowly, so there could be no mistake. "I have a reputation here. Everyone knows me. I can't let people think I'm the town tramp."

"You should have thought of it before you chose your outfit this morning." His gaze started the toes of her boots and glided up her body. "Dominatrix boots and a micro mini. Surely not the average West of Ireland get-up?"

"Look around, Sailor; you've spent too long at sea. What were you expecting, *The Quiet Man?* Things have moved on. Modern women wear *what* they want," she attacked, poking him in the chest with a glossy red fingernail, "*when* they want, and *where* they want. How dare you dictate to me what I should or should not wear?"

"You're having problems being taken seriously. Half of your clients don't trust you and the rest are wasting their energies trying to get a date."

She opened her mouth to protest, and then snapped it shut. He held up a hand in front of her face—like a grouchy teenager.

"Let me finish. You've had your say."

Her eyes blazed, but she remained silent.

"You can't blame them, not when you're dressed like that." He waved a hand at her outfit dismissively. "And while you're *single*, and so obviously *available*, you're a distraction. The guys who are interested in meeting someone and having a relationship are going to be distracted trying to impress you."

"I…"

"You should be thanking me," he growled brutally. "I've taken you off the market, sweetheart. At least for the duration of the festival you're with me, and once everyone in this village understands that, you'll be able to do your job properly."

"What if I don't want to be with you?"

"Then pretend. You want to do the best job for your father. Surely a few days faking a relationship with me is worth that?"

He was right, damn him. If she went back into the pub and told everyone it was all a mistake no one would believe her. Not with the way she'd burst into flames at his kiss. Then walked out the door like a lamb beside him. Her nose wrinkled. If she followed his lead and let this charade continue it would not only put paid to the unwanted male attention she was getting, but also lessen the buzz of female interest he was attracting. Already she'd had to disappoint three women asking if he had signed up for the matchmaking service. If the story got out they were a couple, it would forewarn any lonely hearts looking for love with Sailor Jack. And the story was out, or would be.

"All right, you win." He gaped at her sudden capitulation. He wasn't to know when she was beat Annie replanned and regrouped. "Take me to lunch. I'm going to need something to fortify me. You will too, the minute my mother hears this news."

CONVERSATION STALLED when they walked into the pub an hour later. Jack's arm was casually slung around Annie's shoulders, and the back of his neck prickled at the curious glances aimed their direction. As the very public head of Miller Advertising, he was always starring in the New York tabloids. But this perusal was a lot more personal. He was the man who'd managed to snare the elusive Annie Devine. That earned him grudging respect, apparently.

In New York, people avoided eye contact. In Ireland, eye contact was a national sport. Now he'd caught her it looked like the whole town were going to be a hell of a lot more interested in what happened next.

"Just open up the book, would you Jack? I'm just going to the bathroom."

He set the heavy book down on the table, and flicked it open to a new page. Within minutes, a young man with longish brown hair and an earnest expression sank down onto the chair opposite.

"I'm Noel, Noel McDonagh," he said.

"Annie'll be here to take your details in a minute."

"Ah, she has them already." Noel fidgeted, holding something back.

Jack flicked back through the book until he found Noel's picture.

"Ah yeah, so she does." He scanned the information written in Annie's clear, confident handwriting. The skimpy information revealed the bare bones about her subject, with very little meat.

"So, what's going on?"

Noel's shoulders relaxed from their defensive hunch; a tentative smile played over his lips. "Annie set me up for a date last night, but it was a complete disaster!" His hair stood up at the front as he ran a hand through it. "You know how it is. My date was into cars, fashion, and film stars. I couldn't talk to her at all. I just froze up. I'm speechless around women."

Annie came back into the room. He caught her eye, and shook his head imperceptibly. She raised her eyebrows then joined a couple of girls she obviously knew at a nearby table.

"I know how that can be, Mate. So, what sort of woman do you think you'd like?"

Jack noted Noel's answer, appreciating the other man's gentleness and sense of humor.

"What are your favorite things to do?" Jack asked. "What's your favorite film?" Long years of working in advertising had prepared him perfectly for this. In his business, he had to know a product's strengths and weaknesses so he could properly sell it in the marketplace.

In many ways, matchmaking was a lot like advertising.

Half an hour later, they were finished.

"We'll have a look in the book for a suitable girl. I'll give you a call later on to set up a date for tonight."

"I look forward to hearing from you, Jack." Noel grinned and strolled away; a newly acquired confident swagger attracting a few female glances on the way out.

Annie was there before Noel's chair had gone cold.

"That was amazing," she breathed, admiration shining in her brown eyes. "I couldn't get a word out of him when he was here yesterday."

"He's shy around women. He came to report on last night's date." Her eyebrows rose in hopeful anticipation. "Total disaster. Sorry."

"Win some, lose some." Her mouth drooped at the corners. She played with the hem of her tee- shirt, disappointment evident in every miniscule movement.

"Let's go for win some. We've lost enough." He pointed at the tightly written page of information next to Noel's picture. A line of people was forming. It was time to leave her to do her stuff.

"You're busy, and I have some calls to make. I'm going back to the house. We'll work on Noel later."

Annie reached into her voluminous handbag and dug around for something. "You can take the car if you pick me up later."

"Great." Jack snagged the keys from her upheld fingers. "Knock 'em dead, sweetheart." He leaned close to whisper against her mouth, "Remember, we're supposed to be in love," before he kissed her softly. "I'll see you later."

Swallows swooped low between the trees, performing complex avian choreography in their hunt for insects. Stares on his back prickled like tiny darts thrown at a dartboard as he strode out of the bar. It was going to be an interesting festival all right.

Maeve was on her hands and knees pulling weeds out of the flowerbed as he strode towards the house. "Hello, Jack." She wiped the back of her gloved hand over her damp forehead and leant back on her heels. "Would you like a cup of tea? I'm just about to have one."

"No thanks, Maeve. I've got to do some work." Although how he could concentrate when all the way back to the house he'd replayed the moments alone with Annie in his head, was beyond him. The feel of her body on his when she'd pushed him against the wall, her breasts so soft against the hardness of his chest had aroused him to fever pitch. He'd barely managed to stop himself plundering her lips. Only her anger held him in check. They had to talk before taking things further. He'd said he was kissing her to help her, but it was a lot more personal. It had become so the moment her arms wove around his neck in the pub. Maeve missed nothing. In his current state, God knows what she might winkle out of him.

Jack had a presentation to Bateau Rouge to finish. He powered up his video camera, and rewound to the beginning. Endless blue water and even bluer sky filled the tiny screen. The only sound was the steady slap of waves against the yacht's sides.

At first, the lack of people and sound had been disorientating, but after a few days, it became normality. His view had extended to the blank horizon, while his life contracted to the tight confines of the cabin. He peered at the picture on the screen. Sounds faded away until he was almost back at the helm again. Guiding the little boat through the rough waves of the Atlantic Ocean. His fingers flew over the keyboard, catching the elusive memories and weaving them into his presentation. The final pieces found their places and clicked home like a jigsaw puzzle. He pressed save and leaned back on the chair. He'd nailed it. Now all he had to worry about was the meeting on Monday.

NONE of the men who sat opposite Annie during the afternoon were as interesting as Jack. Not one of them came close. Even when they talked so earnestly about what they were looking for and what they felt they could offer. They smiled and flirted but made no impact. Like a woman behind a Plexiglas screen, she was shielded from the charms of any man but Jack.

"Come outside, and I'll take your picture."

She flicked through the photos on her digital camera. A smile teased her lips at the one up Jack's nostril. She pulled in a deep breath at the picture where he'd stopped glaring, and turned the full wattage of his devastating smile her direction instead.

"Do I smile or should I try looking sexy?" The

tall surfer was gazing at her. Jack had effortlessly managed to do both.

"Just smile." She thumbed the camera into photo mode, and clicked the button.

"That's great, thanks." It was a good picture. The surfer looked smiling and handsome. Her fingers burned to flick back to Jack's face again. She pushed her hair back from her face then smoothed it with rapid fingers behind her ear. "Let's go back inside and finish up."

Jack Miller had taken up residence in her head. She had the funny feeling he'd permeated her bloodstream too, drawn inexorably by the pumping of her inner muscle closer and closer towards her heart.

The golden sun was sinking in the sky and her stomach rumbled. It must be dinnertime. She stuffed the book into her bag and waited outside. After a moment, her car drew up.

"Sorry, I was talking to your mum," Jack explained.

That sounded ominous. She clambered into the passenger seat, holding down the hem of her skirt to keep from revealing all.

"I've only just come out."

His gaze flickered to her legs, and then he leaned over and kissed her quickly. "For our audience," he muttered against her lips before he pulled back. Her heart was racing mile a minute.

God, how was she going to bear this if he kissed her every time they met? She couldn't care about an audience; she wanted to kiss him for real.

"Was she giving you the third degree?"

"No. I don't think she's heard anything yet. We were talking about dinner. I told her I'd like to take you out tonight. Let you show me the sights." He glanced at her thighs again, and she angled her knees towards him.

"Okay, that sounds good." A lot better than sitting with her parents again, anyway. They were going to be curious when they found out, and she couldn't cope with the third degree, not until she'd got her feelings under control.

Jack obviously had a need for speed. He drove with masculine assurance through the cowslip fringed lanes, tanned hands flexing on the wheel he fed through long fingers. She closed her eyes to block out the image, but it was no use. What would those hands feel like sliding over her body? Her nipples formed hard peaks inside the lace of her bra at the mere thought. If he could do this to her without even touching her, she was in real trouble. Her unruly imagination was having a field day.

Annie's nostrils flared with the scent of warm man and hot sun. A delicious combination. She clamped her knees together, willing her treacherous body to behave. Her lungs ached as if she was swimming underwater, desperate to break the surface for air. She clenched her teeth. Crossed her arms over her chest in an attempt to disguise her body's response to him. It wasn't working. If anything, the feel of her arms against her oversensitive breasts heightened her arousal. She wound down the window and looked out at the ocean. A gentle sea breeze played across the tops of the cerulean waves. She breathed it in deeply. Eventually, her breathing returned to normal.

"How was your afternoon?" He was making small talk. She puffed out a breath, relieved.

"Great, actually. A couple I matched last night came in to tell me that their date was a success. They're going out again tonight."

"That's fantastic."

Warmth flooded her, and the tension streamed out of her stiff shoulders.

"Yes. It's a miracle." It had been one small victory in an ocean of defeats. Hardly up to Bull's standards, but better than nothing. The happy couple had left with their arms around each other, and if she hadn't been so tired, she would have done a happy dance.

"So you live in Dublin, most of the time." His gaze remained on the road as he took a corner at breakneck speed.

"Yes. I've lived there for the last couple of

years. I prefer it. I want to make my own way in life away from the village. I've always dreamed of opening a chocolate shop in Dublin. If I win the Chocolate Oscar, I'll be able to. The prizewinner gets a year's free rent at an artisan chocolate shop on Dublin's main shopping street. It's an opportunity of a lifetime and the publicity will be really good for business."

"Don't you miss being at home?" He glanced at her.

"No. I love it. Here, everyone knows my business. In Dublin, I'm just a person in a crowd. I like the anonymity." Her nerves skittered. She changed the subject. "What have you been up to all afternoon?"

"I was working. I have a meeting on Monday in Dublin."

"We'll have to talk to my parents. You need to prepare yourself for the third degree."

She twisted her hands in her lap. Bull and Maeve were so overprotective they'd want to know everything. She was so confused about Jack she didn't want to discuss him with anyone, least of all her parents. The engine slowed. Jack pulled in to a lay-by and turned off the engine.

"You're nervous," he stated flatly. "I don't understand why. You're not a teenager bringing home your first boyfriend." Curious eyes flickered over her. Her heart sank. She had to explain.

"Oh, no. Don't tell me I'm your first boyfriend."

"Of course you're not my first boyfriend. I'm twenty-four, for goodness sake!" What kind of sad creature did he think she was? "You are, however, the first man who's taken me out since the *big disaster*." Silence stretched between them. His gaze was patiently penetrating. She pulled in a deep breath that expanded her chest then puffed it out slowly before continuing.

"Every aspect of my life when I was growing up was an open book. There's no such thing as privacy in such a small village." She worried her lip with her teeth, hating that no matter how she told it she would sound like a victim.

"I fell in love with a boy from the village. Steve Jackson," she admitted flatly. "My father didn't like him. He told me I was making a mistake, but I didn't listen."

It was a hateful story. Even two years later, the betrayal stung.

"He left me at the altar. It was a scandal, especially when we discovered he ran off with another girl from the village." The pain in her chest eased at the understanding and compassion in his azure eyes. Jack wasn't judging her. Unlike the entire village, who acted as though somehow Steve's abandonment was her fault.

"I'm sorry that happened to you. Your fiancé

should have been man enough to tell you before…" He frowned.

"Before our wedding day," she added quietly. "Yes, he should have. I think he just couldn't face telling me. All the preparations were underway, and both our families were so excited." The news had devastated his parents, too. They were the first to console her in the days after.

"Anyway, as a result my parents are justifiably overprotective. By kissing me in the pub today, you've put the entire village on alert. The net curtains are going to be twitching for the next few days, with half the town on *dump watch*." She rubbed damp palms over her skirt.

"I'm sick and tired of being the focus for gossip," she explained. "Everyone will have an opinion. Just you wait and see."

Jack mulled over her words silently, his face a study in concentration. "So, you believe everyone in this town is going to care about how I treat you. To me that sounds like there's a warm and loving community who give a damn about you. I grew up alone, Annie. There are worse things than having people care about you." He reached across the seat and hooked a hand behind her head, pulling her closer.

"Kiss me." His lips moved closer and her heart hammered. "I've been thinking about you all afternoon."

FIVE

Annie's smooth lips parted, allowing him access. Jack dimly registered the taste of lemons as he plundered her mouth hungrily. He angled himself closer in the squashed confines of the car, wishing he could pull her over the space between them into his lap. This was no kiss for spectators. It was all about the two of them. His heart beat a rapid tattoo as he shoved his fingers through her hair, caressing the soft curve of her neck. Her breath was coming as fast as his and things were rapidly getting out of control. He wanted her with an urgency that pole-axed him. His knees banged against the gearshift. They should be somewhere else. Somewhere where they could explore each other's bodies completely. Anywhere but in her tiny car on the way to her family home.

An engine gunned. Jack pulled back, breathing hard, as a small red car rushed past.

What on earth was the matter with him? He'd never been so out of control that he'd wanted to strip a woman bare and make love with her on the side of the road before.

"We ought to get home," Annie muttered, her mouth looking swollen from his kisses.

"Yes." He dropped his hands into his lap. Struggled to get his aroused body back under his control. "This isn't the place for kissing."

"Right." Annie stared out of the window. Every molecule of her body was rigid. She must be feeling raw and exposed after revealing her past to him. What sort of a man was this fiancé, to leave a woman he had to have loved at some stage alone at the altar? Annie might be prepared to cut her ex some slack, but he wasn't. Despite her charitable words, anger flared.

No man deserved to get away so lightly with hurting a woman. Especially not a woman with an open and giving heart like Annie.

He started up the engine. Annie should be angry, not forgiving. He hadn't forgiven Sharon for her betrayal. He'd given Sharon a key to his apartment, never dreaming she'd bring a man there. The day Jack walked into his bedroom and found her writhing on top of a naked stranger had been the day trust died. He'd instantly ordered her out, coldly unmoved by her crying and pleading for another chance. When she'd gone he'd stripped the sheets from the bed and thrown them away, and had replaced the bed the next day. He'd learned his lesson five years ago.

Annie wasn't anything like Sharon. She bore no resemblance to the blonde army either. She was like a locked box he didn't have a key to. Her willingness to forgive was perplexing. He didn't even try to understand. Women were a different species, and whatever he said at this point was bound to be wrong. He pulled out onto the road again, swerving to avoid wheel-breaking potholes. Maybe if he'd grown up differently, with a caring adult to talk to he'd be better at comforting, but he hadn't. Silence stretched between them, like a rubber band forced to the breaking point. With relief, he pulled up outside the house.

Maeve was waiting for them in the kitchen, arms akimbo on rounded hips. "Ah. Here you are Venus Anne Devine. Have you anything to tell me?" Her eagle-eyed glance flicked from Annie to Jack questioningly. God. Talk about out of the frying pan into the fire.

"Venus Anne?" he murmured.

"Venus Anne," she confirmed, through pinched lips.

"What would I have to tell you, Mum?"

"Well, to start with, you could tell me when

you and Jack became an item. The phone's rung off the hook all afternoon."

"Who phoned?" Annie asked wearily.

A headache started to thud in his temples. Annie was right. Kissing someone in the pub was obviously a huge deal in this close-knit community.

"Who hasn't?" The ringing of the phone diverted Maeve's attention for a moment. "You. Don't move!" Maeve pinned Jack and Annie with a glare and answered it. "Hi, Miley...Yes. They're here now. Oh," her eyebrows shot scalpward. "In the car? Right. Well they seem to have sorted out any car trouble they were having...Sure they're here now."

Maeve hung up. "That was Miley. He saw you a couple of minutes ago."

The red car that sped past while they were kissing. Thank God Jack hadn't gone with his body's urgings and slipped his hand under her tee-shirt to stroke her breast. Or skimmed the smooth legs that invited his attentions. They'd probably have the fire engine here to meet them if that was the case. Maybe even the gardai to take him away for lewd behavior.

Annie stood silent beside him. She was probably wondering what to tell her mother. They couldn't really claim it was a sham. Not after Miley's phone call. The situation was beyond ridiculous. She was a grown woman, not a naughty teenager. Jack reached over and squeezed her hand gently. He would handle it.

"I couldn't wait to kiss her until we got here." He moved closer. "We wanted to tell you together." A tentative smile teased the corners of her mouth, and the worry faded from her eyes.

"Annie and I have decided to go on a couple of dates, starting tonight." He smiled back. She wasn't in this, at least, on her own.

Her mother's mouth opened then closed. Her words remaining blissfully unspoken.

AS ANNIE REPORTED on the day's matchmaking, Jack climbed the stairs to the bedroom and powered up his computer. The email was waiting in his in-box: a small collection of words, so ordinary and inconsequential, but monumental nonetheless. *Mrs Mary Byrne, Ivy Nursing Home, 4 King Street, Greystones*. Nothing more, nothing less. The private eye he'd hired before leaving New York had done his job well.

He checked the details again. No telephone number. Anger swelled in his breast, as it had more than once in the years since his parents' death. He pulled out the letter he'd demanded from the agency when he turned eighteen. Pain stabbed at his chest again. Rather than being alone in the world as he always thought, he had a living relative who could have claimed him after the car crash so cruelly took both his young parents' lives.

Mary Byrne is unable to offer her grandson a home. Reading the words hurt as much as it did the first time. Now, years later, he'd found the woman who could have given him a completely different life. He'd endured the foster homes for years, longing for someone to come and claim him. Eventually his innocent optimism had eroded. No one ever would. The only person in the world he could rely on was the one person he spent all his time with, himself.

He closed the laptop breathing heavily in the quiet darkness.

"HE'S THE ONE," Bull declared, elbows on the honey pine table's surface. "I approve. So does your mother."

"Ah, Dad. We've only just met."

"Yes, you've only just met, but there's something strong between you, there's no point denying it. I've years of experience." He slurped his coffee, swallowing his final antibiotic for the day with it. "I'm feeling better. I'll have the pills finished in a couple of days."

Annie eyed him critically. His color was better; the sparkle, which had dimmed his eyes over the past week, was back.

"Well, I like him." The words rang with truth. Jack was amusing and interesting. She certainly found him attractive. A forest fire raced through her every time their eyes met. He was also amazingly skilled at dealing with her parents. He'd answered some of Maeve's questions, and deflected others. All without causing offence, or finding himself pinned on the spot. It was a skill she'd yet to master. Her parent's beady-eyed regard always immobilized her like a butterfly pinned to a velvet board.

"He had a real rapport with Noel McDonagh." She showed him the page full of details. "They just sat and chatted for ages."

"Where were you?"

"I sat it out in the back of the pub."

Bull nodded his approval. "Some men are so shy they're better talking to other men. That's just the way of it. Maybe if Jack's around for the next couple of days he might help out again?"

"I'm sure he might. We want to organize a date for Noel tonight. Who do you think?"

She successfully diverted her father from his

new favorite topic, Jack Miller. Soon they had drawn up a brief list of potential dates.

"Why don't you ask Jack for his opinion?" Bull asked. "After all, he spent all the time with Noel."

"Right." She climbed the stairs to the bedroom and tapped lightly on the door, wondering at the lack of light seeping from underneath. *He couldn't have gone out, could he?*

The door jerked open.

"Annie." The soft rumble of his voice turned her knees to jelly. He hauled her in, backing her up against the wall and kissing her hungrily. Her heart thundered in her chest at the assault of his lips on hers. His hands ran up and down her arms. It was too fast, unexpected. She pushed against his chest, forcing him back.

"What are you doing?"

Jack stepped back, running a hand through his hair.

"You kissed me in the car, I thought…"

"You thought what?"

Blood heated her face. She'd told him all her secrets. Had exposed her core. The balance had shifted between them after her confession. Did he pity her? Was that what this was about, a mercy roll in the hay?

"Did you think I was coming in here to tumble into bed with you?" A potent mix of anger and vulnerability rippled through her. She yearned to feel the heat of his body against hers again, but her mind rioted at the thought. She couldn't resist Jack. The knowledge scared her silly. There was no way in hell she was going down this road again. She'd been there, done that. Never again would she fall for a man who would walk away, leaving her behind.

"Yes." Stormy indigo eyes clashed and blazed. "There's something between us. I feel it, and so do you."

"An attraction." She bit her lip, admitting it. "I know. I shouldn't have let you kiss me in the car. I'm not in the market for a relationship, and neither are you. We barely know each other."

"What's to stop us getting to know each other better?" His arms fell to his sides.

"Good sense, for one thing." She pushed a lock of hair behind her ear. "We will pretend to be falling in love, but I'm not fooling myself. Anything between us would be temporary, and then you'd be headed home again. It will be easier to face the pitying glances if I'm not really dumped."

"So what did you really come up here for?" His jaw clenched tightly in the light spilling into the room from the open door.

"Dad asked me to get you. To look at the list of dates we've chosen for Noel."

He strode to the window and stared out,

tension evident in the set of his shoulders. "Tell him I'll be down in a moment."

"Jack."

He turned to her. "I'm in no fit state to go downstairs, Annie. I need some time alone. I'll be down in a minute."

He walked to her and grasped her arm. Words froze in her throat as he propelled her to the door and nudged her through it.

THE DOOR CLICKED CLOSED behind her and Jack escaped to the window again, staring out into the darkened garden with sightless eyes.

Dammit, she had him tied up in knots. He'd never been so attracted. He was so out of control around her it was like being a teenager again. When he'd seen her standing in the doorway he hadn't been able to stop reaching for her. Kissing her. He breathed out heavily. He'd behaved like a Neanderthal. He pushed his fingers through his hair. His rioting body remembering the feel of her, and her taste. Pretending to be her lover would be hell. A summer fling in Ireland might be exactly what he needed, but Venus Anne Devine didn't do *casual.* Her response just now had proved that. Casual was all he could offer; he sure wasn't in the market for a relationship, no matter how attractive the package.

He clumped noisily down the stairs to the kitchen. Pushing open the door, he bit back a savage grin at the three faces turned his direction. If he hadn't known better, he would have sworn they were talking about him.

"Jack, we've a couple of ideas of a match for Noel. Come and let us know what you think."

He pulled up a chair, and swiveled the book around to face him. "Tell me about them. Noel was pretty definite about the sort of woman that interested him, let's see if any of these meet the bill."

It was surprisinglyeasy to decide on a candidate. A pretty girl who had recently moved to the area, and was beset with acute shyness.

"I'll call them and set it up." Annie picked the phone off the wall.

"I'll talk to Noel," Jack suggested. "I told him I'd call."

"Right." She dialed the number and passed the phone over. Her brow creased in concentration, and she listened to their easy banter with rapt attention.

"Right, you call Annabel now." He passed Annie the phone. "So she'll be expecting Noel's call."

There was a touch of pink high in her cheeks

when she talked to Noel's intended. Her long slender fingers fiddled with a pen. Her leg jiggled with unspent energy.

She's nervous, she finds talking to people difficult. He struggled with the idea, but giving it headspace, realized it was true. All the markers were there in their earlier encounters, but since they'd spent their time either disagreeing or kissing, he hadn't picked up on how uncomfortable she was talking to people. She had been as caught up as he was upstairs, but for some reason denied it.

The conversation over, she replaced the phone in its cradle on the wall, and returned to the table. "She's ready." Annie's excitement was infectious. "I think it's going to work. They seem a good match."

"Well done, Annie." Bull patted her arm. "Now, what have you two got planned for the evening?"

"I'm taking Jack to check out the village nightlife. I just need to change first." No more tempting legs then. The thought was oddly depressing. She turned her chocolate gaze to him. "I'll be down in a couple of minutes."

SHE PARKED in a tree-lined square up the hill from the restaurant they'd lunched in. People were everywhere. They sat on benches under the leafy chestnut trees and at tables outside bars and cafes. Music swelled from open doorways, drifting on the warm evening breeze. It all made for a cosmopolitan scene. Not one he'd imagined finding on Ireland's west coast.

"We have thousands of visitors during the festival. It's the biggest event of the year." Annie strolled toward a café. "The food's good here."

He nodded, and she bagged the last available table and sank onto a chair.

"How long has the festival been running?"

"About forty years. In the early days it was all about the matchmaking, now it's the perfect excuse for everyone to get together and have a good time." She brushed her hair back from her animated face. "A ceili is organized by the community council." She laughed at his confused expression. "That's a dance, Jack. Everyone goes."

He nodded, enjoying the flirtatious note in her voice.

"There is a film festival in the cinema, and all the bars and restaurants offer festival specials. It's a great place to be for a couple of weeks."

"I fell on my feet then, arriving when I did."

"Well, you won't find a better time in any town in Ireland. Not this week anyway." She grinned, gazing out at the couples, who strolled with arms around each other in the square.

A waiter approached with two menus. Jack ordered a bottle of Chianti to start the evening off, and glanced at the food on offer.

"The risotto is to die for."

"Two." Jack ordered. Her eyes glowed in reflected lights strung along the café's awning. Warm, inviting.

"So, tell me about your work."

"I work in advertising. I have a potential client I'm giving a presentation to in Dublin on Monday. I have a few other small things to take care of while I'm here." Small things. What an understatement. Finding the woman who'd rejected him was one of the biggest things he'd ever done.

"An airplane would be faster," she teased, leaning closer. She'd changed into jeans and a sparkly top, which revealed acres of creamy cleavage. His gaze dipped, until he dragged it up to her mouth.

"Yes, it would. But the client I'm meeting has a special interest in sailing, so it made more sense to sail." He grinned. "And I love the sea, so…any excuse."

"You need to follow your passions." It was one of those loaded comments. His current passion was Annie, he'd made that only too clear. He picked up the wineglass and drank. If she wanted him, she'd have to be clearer. He wasn't putting himself on the line for rejection again.

The waiter arrived with flat dishes of creamy risotto topped with slivers of parmesan. He picked up a fork and started eating.

"Tell me about your people, Jack. Where are your parents from?"

Jack swallowed. Even after so many years, he couldn't talk about his past without pain piercing his chest like a dagger. "My parents are both dead," he answered flatly. "But they were Irish."

"I'm sorry." Annie's eyes were full of compassion. "That must be hard for you."

"It was a long time ago." She was silent, waiting for more. There wasn't any. Talking about his childhood would be a complete downer.

"I've moved on."

"This must all seem alien after New York." She forked a mouthful of risotto into her mouth and chewed.

"Yeah, it's different all right. A lot quieter." Her small pink tongue darted out to swipe a morsel of rice from her top lip. His core blazed with awareness at the tiny movement.

He covered her hand with his, and her pupils expanded at the touch of his flesh on hers. She stilled, staring at him. A passing girl who'd had too much to drink, bumped against the table, jolting it. The interruption broke the mood stretched tight like the fairy lights above.

"I have an apartment in Manhattan, and an office downtown." Cold, empty and sterile. He walked past thousands of people everyday. Thousands of strangers.

Not so here. Passing people smiled. Some said hello, some didn't. The vast majority acknowledged Annie in some way. It was a potent reminder of the connection he was missing. The one he'd come half way across the world to discover.

"I'd love to see New York." There was a wistful note in her voice. "I haven't traveled at all, apart from a brief holiday in France with a couple of friends. Steve and I were going to go to Australia on our honeymoon." She eased her hand away, and picked up her glass. "He took Elaine instead. I think that's the bit that hurt most!"

Her smile hid the truth he glimpsed in eyes suddenly lowered. It wasn't just the stolen honeymoon, but the stolen husband that hurt.

A rush of jealous anger flooded him. He didn't want to think of Annie with another man, or mooning over one, either. "Do you still think of him?" The words ground out of him before he realized it. She raised her eyes to his and her mouth gaped a little.

He knew it wasn't any of his business. He didn't have any right to question her about her ex. She swallowed.

"I thought you were in advertising, not therapy." Her smile didn't quite reach her eyes.

"You said you hadn't dated since him."

"I've been out with a couple of men in Dublin, but nothing serious." She was silent for a moment, and then pulled in a breath. "I don't think of Steve anymore. For a long time I wondered what I did wrong. I agonized over why he chose Elaine instead of me. After a while, I decided we just wanted different things. I'm better off without him. I just wish I didn't have to deal with the fallout."

"How long ago was the *disaster*?"

She bit her bottom lip.

"Two years. You'd think our neighbors would have moved on, but it's still talked about. Mum got asked how I was coping just last week." A bitter smile twisted her mouth. "I guess they don't know because I don't live here anymore. I only come home for Christmases, really."

It was inconceivable she'd let one bad experience drive her away from home and loving family. Could she really not see what she had?

"What about your family?"

She shrugged. "I'm only a couple of hours away. If there's a problem I can get here quickly."

She changed the subject. "What about you, Jack? Is there anyone special waiting for you back in New York?" Cool, calm, collected. Her fingers worried her napkin. She carefully tore the flimsy paper into strips. Despite her cool words, she cared what his answer would be.

"No. I'm unattached. I wouldn't have kissed you in the pub if I was seeing someone."

She leant back on the cane chair. "Was there anyone?" she whispered.

"There was. A long time ago." He'd probed her secrets, and owed her the truth. "We weren't engaged, but I'd been thinking about it. It didn't work out." He'd never told anyone the full details of Sharon's betrayal, but Annie had been so honest he had to reciprocate. "I came home unexpectedly one day and found her in my bed with someone else. That was the end of that."

"I'm sorry." Her expressive eyes confirmed it.

"It was a long time ago. I'm over it."

Love brought nothing but heartache. It was a hard lesson he'd learnt with his parents' death. And he'd had it burned into him again when he found Sharon in bed with another man. Annie must have learnt that lesson too, after being left at the altar. Love wasn't worth it. It was better to have a relationship where both parties knew the score. Friends with benefits. No broken hearts involved.

The waiter cleared their plates.

"I don't want anything else. I'm still full after that lunch you bought me."

After he settled the bill, she stood and pulled him to his feet. "Come on, let's have a look around."

His yacht tied up on the jetty was just visible from the brow of the hill. He pointed the small white craft out to her in the sea washed silver by the moon's light. The muted hum of people and music drifted up to them from their vantage point above the town.

"You had no one to talk to for weeks at sea. How did you survive?"

Moonlight painted the face tilted towards his with its silvery glow. Chestnut highlights glistened in its light. She barely came up to his shoulder, and he resisted a primitive urge to put a protective arm around her.

"I liked being alone. Plenty of time to think." The thoughts had come thick and fast on the solitude of the water. Like the eddies in the yacht's wake, they'd swirled around him constantly. Thoughts of his grandmother, and what his future might be when he found her.

"I would have gone crazy, out there all alone." She shivered.

"I didn't feel alone." He was following in the watery wake of every sailor who had gone before.

The trivial worries of day-to-day living had faded away, replaced with joy at the occasional sight of a school of fish, or the birds landing on deck, catching a ride. It was a purer, alternative view of life. One where he felt truly alive. The wonder of the voyage had permeated his psyche, changing him forever.

A smile curved his lips, remembering.

"It was a wonderful experience, wasn't it?" She didn't press him for details, just reached for his hand, squeezing it gently.

"Yes."

She trailed a finger across his cheek, and then reached up for him, teasing his lips with hers briefly before pulling back.

"What was that for?"

"Just because I wanted to. Come on, I want to show you something."

THEY WALKED BACK toward the car. People were everywhere, holding hands, kissing. Taking a chance on love. All day long she'd told people to open their hearts and be brave. What a hypocrite. Jack climbed into the passenger seat next to her and put on his seatbelt. She hadn't felt this powerful attraction for two years, hell, she was even more attracted than she'd ever been to Steve.

And how had she reacted? She'd done her best to push him away. It was time to stop running.

She turned off the main road down a track that led to a hidden strand. Flecks of mica in the sand glittered, lighting their way. Tufts of spiky grass sprouted from the dunes, rustling secrets in the breeze. The waves were dark stripes in the silver ebb and flow of the water. The engine's sound faded to silence.

"It's beautiful."

"I thought you'd like it." They climbed from the car and leant on the car's hood. The warm breeze teased her hair. The night air was infused with the scent of tangy salt and seaweed. She licked her lips, tasting the salt on her tongue.

"I'm sorry about earlier. In your room."

"I was out of line." He crossed his arms.

"No. I was just taken by surprise, that's all." She stepped in front of him. Slid a hand up his chest. "Things escalated so quickly between us…"

His jaw was set in a forbidding line. "What are you saying, Annie?"

"I'm saying I feel this attraction between us, too." Wind whispered through the grasses on the dunes. His chest was hard under her hands. Unyielding.

"You were right. I'm not going to be around. No matter how things go, I've a life in New York. I'm not the settling down kind."

"I never asked you to settle down." He'd somehow cast her in the role of needy spinster in need of a husband. Anger bubbled. Erupted. "You've some cheek thinking I would even want to settle down. I've only known you for a couple of days."

"You're not the type for a quick fling." It was the truth, and she was furious he'd read her so easily.

"How do you know that?" She shook her head. Didn't he feel the heat between them? Wasn't he feeling out of control too? Her whole body was in uproar, yearning for his touch. She was sick and tired of taking the safe option. Right now, a dangerous fling with Jack was more than something she wanted. It was something she needed, with every fiber of her body.

"I know you're not a woman to love and leave. A relationship between us would be a bad idea."

"Why don't you stop thinking, and let me decide what's good for me?" Love and leave would be a hell of a lot more satisfying than just leave. She'd been left before. This time was different. This time she was the one calling the shots.

"You've seen one side of me, Jack. It's the side my parents see. Small village Annie. There's a big city Venus you've yet to meet."

She'd never tried to seduce anyone before. Had always been the prey, rather than the hunter.

This time was different. She wanted him. In a slow slide, she moved closer, liking the way his eyes darkened at her approach. She wound an arm around the back of his neck, and dragged him down to her, kissing him hard.

His hands slipped under the hem of her top and held her close. Warm lips kissed her back. He muttered against her mouth. "This is not a good idea." His fingers stroked her skin under the soft cotton.

"I think it's an excellent idea." She snuggled closer. The hard evidence of his arousal nudged against her stomach. His lips trailed from mouth to neck. She shivered. The sensation of his mouth on her skin was sending her body into uproar. He worked his way up to her lips again, tongue tracing her bottom lip, before plundering her mouth again. She arched into his kiss, heart hammering. Desperate to get closer. His hands cupped her bottom pulling her against his hard arousal.

"There's a blanket in the boot." She barely recognized her husky voice. Hell, she barely recognized the wanton siren as herself either, but somehow she'd managed to convince Jack she was serious. There was no way she was going to slow things down now.

"I want to be in a warm bed, with crisp white

sheets, and you," he murmured. "I don't want our first time to be here."

"But it's so beautiful. It has everything. Moon, water, solitude…"

"Let's not forget sand and the possibility of being caught in the act," he finished. Easing his body away. His thumb brushed her bottom lip. "We need to slow things down; take our time." Like a thrown bucket of icy water, his words chilled her to the bone. Her hands fell to her sides and she shivered.

"You're cold. We should get back."

She couldn't look at him, couldn't speak. *Couldn't she do anything right?* Unskilled at seduction, her brave attempt had gone horribly wrong. With a frozen heart she climbed into the car. The moonlit beach bearing silent witness to her humiliation.

SIX

A rap on the door jolted Annie from a fevered dream. In it, she stood shivering on the beach naked in front of a fully dressed Jack. With a shuttered gaze, he'd climbed into the car, and reversed away. Her heart was racing, and her body was sticky with a thin layer of sweat. Her stomach pitched and rolled, churning with nausea.

"Annie, phone!" She forced bleary eyes open. Maeve loomed over her, brandishing the phone like a weapon.

"Thanks Mum." It was only a dream. His rejection hadn't been quite that brutal.

Maeve handed over the phone and bustled out. Annie pulled in a shuddering breath to steady her shredded nerves and clutched the phone in a death grip.

"Hello?"

"Anne Devine?"

"That's me." Light bled in from the gap in the curtains. She blinked at the bedside clock. Who on earth was phoning at half eight on a Saturday morning?

"This is Susan Goff." A pregnant pause. Was she supposed to know Susan Goff? "From the Chocolate Oscars."

Annie shot up in bed with a gasp. Unbelievable. After two weeks totally focused on the Artisan Chocolate competition, she'd forgotten the name of the head judge.

"Miss Goff, of course. Good morning." She regrouped. Pulled up the covers and crossed her fingers. This was it. Was she in, or was her dream about to dissolve like a sugar lump in hot tea? She clamped her eyes shut.

"I'm calling to let you know we loved your Almond Praline Truffle, Miss Devine. You're through to the next stage."

"The finals?" She couldn't breathe. Her eyes shot open, and her heart was pounding in her chest as if it wanted to burst out and dance around the room.

"We'll need your entry in by Sunday evening."

Through a haze of delight, Annie squeaked her thanks to Susan Goff for the call. She hung up. Euphoria fizzed like champagne in her veins.

At least something's going right. She snuggled down in the bed and yanked the duvet up to her chin, luxuriating in the warm glow of success. Determined to make the moment last before she had to get up and greet the day.

THE RAPPING on Annie's door shot Jack from sleep to full alertness. His eyes darted around the unfamiliar room in panic and his muscles tensed ready for flight. In the grey light, he reached over and switched on the bedside lamp.

A painting hung above the worn chest of drawers: a thickly painted rocky outcrop with tiny, fluffy pink flowers protruding from cracks in the stone. He was in Ireland. Finally home in the country his parents had come from, the country where his grandmother still lived.

His heartbeat slowed as reality chased away the bad memories. *It was only a dream.* His legs were tangled in the sheets and he tugged them free. Starved lungs pulled in a deep breath of steadying air. *He was an adult now. An adult with nothing to fear.* Not a kid scared of the dark anymore. He flung back the bedding and strode to the window to pull back the faded curtain.

Annie was so lucky. She had everything he'd always wanted, yet all she wanted was escape. If he had a family like hers, he'd move heaven and earth to keep it.

The memory of her face in the moonlight burned as he forced his hands through tousled hair. He'd totally screwed up last night, pulling away. His heart had plummeted into his shoes the minute she turned away from him. And afterwards, she couldn't get away from him quickly enough. Had darted upstairs and closed the door. Annie wasn't just any woman. Even though she'd told him she was a big City Venus, he didn't believe it for a moment. She was special. He didn't want a quick moment on the beach on a musty blanket; he wanted their lovemaking to be perfect.

The house was not an option, with her parents in the next room. And his boat was a dirty mess after weeks at sea. He couldn't make love to her there. She hadn't understood; had thought he didn't want her. He got that. But fixing it wasn't going to be easy. He snagged his clothes from the chair and got dressed.

There was a hell of a day ahead. He wanted to get into Galway and pick up the car, and then drive to the nursing home. He'd come to Ireland to find out why his grandmother had decided against offering him a home when his parents died. The need for the answer consumed him.

Annie's door creaked open, followed by the

staccato tapping of steps running down the stairs. Last night had been a disaster, but today was a new day, with new opportunities. He'd start with coffee, and take it from there.

———————

ANNIE HELPED herself to two slices of warm soda bread then passed the plate to Jack. Her body buzzed with restless energy, and she could barely sit still. She buttered the slices carefully, watching the butter soften and melt in the scant moments before her mother sat down.

"I've some news." The room fell silent.

"My chocolates have won the next stage. I made the finals!" The words tumbled into the void then the room exploded with excited chatter. Congratulations from her mother punctuated by a playful but hard thump on the arm by her father. "I have to get my entry in by tomorrow night."

"Divine?"

"Yes, my pièce de résistance." Her heart expanded with happiness. She grinned. "I'll have to go back to the flat today and make them."

"But darling, the festival…" Maeve's voice faltered mid-sentence. A myriad of emotions flickered across her face in rapid succession. Pride her daughter had won her dearest goal. Then worry, because her husband might regain his matchmaker role before he was completely better. She could read her mother like a book. Everyone could.

"I can stand in for her, Maeve. I know what needs to be done," Jack said.

"I thought you were busy…" Hadn't Jack said he had work to do this weekend? The presentation he'd crossed the world to make was on Monday. Worry gnawed at Annie's gut.

"I have the time." He took her hand in his and squeezed. She didn't want him touching her. Didn't think she could take it, after the rejection of the night before. She tried to discreetly ease her hand away but he gripped tighter. Unwilling to make a scene, she capitulated and left it there. "You just concentrate on winning the competition."

He was the most confusing person she'd ever met. Hot, then cold. Maybe it was for the best if they kept things cool between them.

Maeve's face softened in relief.

"I can do it," Bull blustered. "It's only for a few days and I've finished the antibiotics…"

"Why not split it then?" Jack seemed to understand Bull's need to be involved. It was his vocation after all. "What time do you have to be at the pub, Annie?"

"Well, there's a 'get to know you' session this morning at the café, and I've organized all the dates for that, so I wasn't due to open up until five o'clock."

Jack released her hand to reach for his coffee. "I have to pick a car up in Galway. If you drop me on the way to Dublin, I'll make my own way back by five. I can finish my work this evening and push my errand out till tomorrow."

"I can do tomorrow, then." Bull happily filled his bread with a couple of rashers and bit in hungrily. All Annie's problems were dissolving one by one. Damn, this day was just getting better and better.

"It'll just be the evening session anyway." Annie smiled at her mother.

"Right, that's sorted," Maeve agreed. "You'd better get yourself ready, Annie, if you're heading back. Have you everything you need?"

"I have all the ingredients and my equipment ready to go back at the flat. I got totally prepared just in case." She swallowed the last fragment of sandwich and drained her teacup. "Can you be ready in half an hour, Jack?"

"Make it fifteen minutes. Thanks for the breakfast, Maeve."

There was something new in Jack's eyes as he pulled his lanky frame from the table. Something hot. It burned to her toes. He glanced away, breaking the spell.

"We better get going." Annie followed him

upstairs, shamelessly taking advantage of the opportunity to check out his rear view in his faded jeans. It was only when he walked into his own room that the sensual fog began to clear.

Clothes and shoes landed haphazardly into her overnight bag. Jack was talking on his mobile next door; the deep rumble of his voice audible through the wall. She should be concentrating on the Chocolate Oscar. The thought of winning had consumed her for months. Instead, thoughts of Jack filled her head.

She couldn't believe how easily he'd diffused the situation downstairs, offering to stand in for her at the festival, and she hadn't even thanked him. She picked up her hairbrush from the dressing table, and threw it in on top of the creased collection of clothes. Time apart was probably a good idea.

"I HAVE to pick the car up from Murphy's Car Hire in Galway. Do you know where it is?" Jack asked. The miles were rapidly gobbled up as they sped down the motorway.

"Yes. That's one of the big ones. It's in the city-center."

"They say they have branches all over."

"Yes, they do. When you're finished with the car you'll be able to drop it anywhere."

She struggled to sound sophisticated and casual. As if the prospect of his leaving meant nothing. She scrunched up her true feelings, and stuffed them into the hole pain was burning into the centre of her chest.

"Trying to get rid of me?" he teased.

"No, but I know you have things to do." She gazed steadily ahead, veiling her turbulent emotions. "Thanks for helping Dad out."

"I'm in no hurry to leave," he answered lazily.

"Is your mobile in your bag?"

She nodded, and he reached for it. "I'm going to put my number in so you can call me. You'll want to know how things go while you're away."

He was right. Despite her initial trepidation, she had built a good rapport with some of their clients. She was itching to know how Noel's date with Annabel had gone.

"Thanks. You'll need to give Dad a report tonight. Especially if he's going to be back on duty tomorrow…"

"Why are you so nervous?" His voice was a low murmur in the quiet car.

"I'm not nervous." She shrugged, and glanced in the rear view mirror. "I don't know what gave you that idea. Dad will be grateful of your presence tonight anyway. He's always hoping for a bit of male companionship on Saturdays."

"You'd better explain that," he replied dryly. "Your father doesn't seem the type."

"Jack!" Her dimples flashed as she glanced his direction, shaking her head at his expression. "You're an evil man. And him a matchmaker."

"Well, what did you mean when you said your father's hoping for male company?"

"Saturday night," she paused for effect, "is LADIES night. During the festival, Mum can't get out to the pub with the girls, because it's the last place a decent, married woman should be. Instead, the ladies come to our house."

"You're leaving me alone with all these ladies?"

"Not one of them is your type." She was confident of that. The average age of the women who frequented ladies night was sixty-five.

"I'm completely confident leaving you in their company. You'll be eating in the sitting room with Dad, while they take over the kitchen. That's the way it normally goes. Men one place, women another. If I was there I'd be in the kitchen with them, but there's matters discussed during ladies night," she dropped her voice to a whisper, "that shouldn't reach the ears of ANY man."

"Sounds terrifying."

"Believe me, it is. I'm just sorry I won't be there to see it."

"See what?"

"The first time the ladies get an up close and personal look at 'my boyfriend'." She shook her head. "On second thoughts I'm SO glad I get to avoid that. By the time they meet again the festival will be old news, and..." *So will we.* The end of the sentence sounded like a death knell in her mind.

"We'll be spending some quality time getting to know each other," he finished.

———

THE WORDS SHOT straight from heart to mouth, bypassing brain altogether. He'd meant to ease into it, not potentially startle her into causing a traffic accident.

"What?" She stared at the road ahead. They passed a 'Galway city center' signpost on the left.

"I was hoping you might show me around Dublin. After the festival is over, of course."

The scent of Annie teased his nostrils. A subtle mix of warm woman tinged with citrus. Her warm body was near, if he edged closer a fraction their bodies would be touching. It was intoxicating. Electricity arced between them.

"You made your feelings clear last night, Jack.

I don't think spending time together in Dublin is a good idea."

"There's the car rental place."

Annie pulled into a shopping center parking lot and turned off the engine.

He had to say it right. Screwing up again wasn't an option. "You thought I rejected you last night. You were wrong." She stared out of the window, effectively blocking him out. He dragged in a ragged breath and blundered on. "I wanted you last night. Couldn't sleep for wanting you." He grasped the hands she twisted in her lap. "I'm not a kid anymore. I wanted more than a stolen moment on a blanket. I wanted…damn it, *want*, more. I want you in my bed. Without the fear of interruption from your mother. That's why I turned away from you last night, not because I wanted to, but because I wanted *more*."

She sat silently. Her usually expressive face shuttered, revealing nothing of her inner thoughts. Desperation threatened to overwhelm him. Was he too late?

He'd never put his feelings out there before. Turning her down had almost killed him. She'd unveiled her attraction last night when she glided close to kiss him. His mind filled with an image of her in his apartment, lying across his big brass bed, hair fanned out around her on the pillow.

She cleared her throat. "I don't know." Doubts swirled in her chocolate eyes.

"If you're not interested, I'll leave you alone." Being needy was something new. His cards were right out there on the table. A tight band crushed his chest as he steeled for the moment when she'd dash them to the floor.

"I am interested. That's the problem." Her mouth curved in a tremulous smile and warm fingers curled around his. "I just don't see where this is going."

His fears dissolved in a hot torrent of relief. "I have no idea either. This is new for me too." He kissed the compelling temptation of her soft pink mouth. "We are, however, straight on one thing, we both want to find out."

Her lips melted under his and parted cautiously. Soft hands crept up his chest and tangled in his hair. The kiss blazed like a forest fire, totally out of control. Before it completely overwhelmed him, he edged away, breathing heavily.

"I'll come up to Dublin tomorrow. Keep your evening open, I'm taking you to dinner."

"And dessert afterward?" She grinned, her elusive dimple making a rare appearance.

"Double helpings." He held up his hand as if swearing he was telling the truth before a judge, and nodded solemnly. Her laughter sparked his answering chuckle. "I'll walk down from here." He climbed out of the car with her to pull his duffel bag out of the back. His hands stroked urgent caresses up and down her arms, unable to resist, loving the feel of her soft skin against his palms.

"See you tomorrow."

"I'll be ready." She climbed back into the car and reversed out of the parking spot. Her eyes met his for a brief moment in the rear view mirror, and then she gunned the engine, and vanished into the mid-morning traffic.

SEVEN

A potent aroma assailed his nostrils as he eased the glass door of the car rental shop open. New car smell, blended with the scent of polish. A receptionist perched behind a large gleaming pine desk. Her eyes flickered over his battered deck shoes and faded clothing as he strode toward her. Her mouth quivered in distaste. "Can I help you?"

He guessed what she was thinking, that in order to have a million dollars, you must look a million dollars. Normally, such a blinkered view irritated. He knew the truth. Those who look a million dollars were usually struggling behind the scenes to scrape together enough cash to cover their rent. Today, her barely concealed expression of horror at having an unshaven sailor in her pristine showroom made no dent at all on his mood. Insulated from irritation as he was by the warm glow of his last conversation with his favorite chocolatier.

"I believe you have a car ready for me," he explained calmly. "Jack Miller?"

Her jaw dropped so comically he had to bite on the inside of his lip to stop from smiling. "Jack Miller?" She blinked.

"That's me." He fished in the back pocket of his faded jeans for his driving license. A graphite grey Aston Martin DBS V12 sat in splendid isolation at the front of the showroom. "Is that it?"

"I'll call Mr. Murphy."

She swiveled on Cuban heels and disappeared. Jack strolled over to the two-door coupe, running a loving hand over the car's curves. *Just like mine, even the same color, Casino Ice.*

A door creaked, and then a balding middle-aged man appeared, hand outstretched. "Mr. Miller. We were expecting you."

"Mr. Murphy." His hand slid off the car's sleek exterior.

"I have the keys all ready for you." Murphy's grip was damp and limp. The sensation was like holding a dead fish. Jack dropped it as soon as was polite. "Your secretary has organized all the paperwork; it's ready to drive away."

The Aston was perfect for the smooth

unblemished streets of New York. Durna had no such streets. The ride was harsh at the best of times over the country roads pitted with potholes. Parked outside the pink house by the sea, the car would be an oddity. He could only imagine the curious looks it would garner from the locals. Annie was sensitive about people gossiping, and the Aston would definitely be a talking point. Such a talking point the entire village would make the pilgrimage.

"Maybe I won't take the Aston Martin."

Murphy's eyes widened in shock. His mouth gaped and he looked so dismayed Jack almost relented. Then an image of Annie filled his mind. She would be happier with something less flashy. More practical. What would please Annie was a factor he hadn't had to consider when he ordered the Aston. Now, it was of major importance. He stuck to his guns.

"It's a beautiful car, and I know you've gone to great lengths to get it for me. You had to bring it in from your Dublin branch, I believe?"

"We did." Murphy crossed his hands over his chest. He still looked upset. As though Jack's rejection had struck him to the core.

"Well, I'm more than happy to cover the extra expenses, but I'm going to need a more conventional car." His gaze settled on a dark blue

BMW coupe. "How about the BMW? Is it available?"

"It is." Murphy dropped his arms to his sides, recovering quickly from the shock of having his baby rejected.

"I have a bit of shopping to do, so I'll fill in all the paperwork now, and then come and collect it when I've finished."

"Right."

Jack dropped into a local café for a cappuccino and a huge pain au chocolate, dunking it like a kid. He still had a rake of things to do. A flood in the cabin had destroyed his work suit. Tomorrow was Judgment Day. The day he'd finally meet his grandmother. Although bruised inside by her lack of interest, there was no way he would show it. Her neglect hadn't damaged him. His hands clenched around the cup, and he drained it rapidly. He was a success. He just needed to look the part.

A pretty waitress sidled over to clear the table. "Hi."

At his greeting, her face flushed red, matching her hair.

"I need to find a man's shop, somewhere I can get a good suit. And a barber. Is there anywhere around here?"

"Magill's is just around the corner," she answered huskily. "You should be able to get whatever you're looking for in there. And the barber is a few shops down." She smiled, flirting. Jack was well aware of his effect on women. Hell, he'd had them falling at his feet for years. None had cracked his veneer. Except Annie. One kiss from her, and he'd shattered.

An hour later, he was at the barber. He had a charcoal grey suit, shoes and all the trimmings in a bag with some new sailing clothes. In the shop he'd changed into new black jeans, a black shirt, and a brown leather jacket with black boots. He'd abandoned his old, worn clothes and shoes. They'd served their purpose.

After a wet shave, he pushed back a lock of hair that dipped into his eyes. His surfer look was at odds with his smooth jaw and his new wardrobe.

The barber stood with scissors poised. "Now, what will we do with this hair?"

"Take it all off." Jack slouched confidently in the chair as the barber set to work. Watching with satisfaction as Jack Miller, millionaire and advertising executive re-emerged.

A vision of Annie as he'd last seen her flooded his thoughts. She didn't know how lucky she was to have a family who cared about her, a place to belong. She was loved and needed. A vital part of the intricate puzzle that formed a family. He'd been part of a family once. Long ago, before his parents were stolen away in the car crash. He hadn't realized how much he'd missed it until her family had embraced him as one of their own.

Meeting Mary Byrne would be hard. He didn't want to prejudge her, but couldn't help it. She was his blood. But she was also the woman who could have given him a home, and instead had left him to take his chances.

Outside the barbers, there were visions of love everywhere. Couples sat on the grass with arms around each other and lay entwined in the rare Irish summer sunshine. He ached to lie there with arms full of Annie. To bury his face in the fragrant cloud of her hair, and trail his lips over her soft neck. He glanced at his watch and cut through the laneway toward the car dealership. He would have to get a move on if he was going to get back to Durna in time for five.

JACK FISHED the black book and Annie's camera from the rucksack, and ambled into the pub. In the early evening's warmth people lounged outside, gazing at the azure sea. Many of them greeted him by name.

"Like the haircut," Niall said from behind the bar. "You look different."

"I've a business meeting in Dublin tomorrow. I

thought I better brush up a bit. Annie's in Dublin today, so I'm in charge." He tapped the book. "For what it's worth."

"A couple of girls came in earlier. I told them the matchmaker would be in at five. You only have a couple of minutes. Can I get you something?" Niall wiped the counter with a beer towel, flicked out new beer mats like a croupier dealing cards.

Jack nodded. "A coffee, please, Niall. I think I better keep my wits about me."

"Good idea." He glanced toward the door.

"Oh, here we go. You're on." A couple of young women lingered in the doorway, then linked arms and approached nervously. They looked as terrified as Jack felt. When they reached him, they stopped and looked him up and down.

Niall gifted them with his best, friendly bartender smile. "Welcome back, ladies. This is Jack. He's standing in for our regular matchmaker, Annie Devine for tonight."

"Hi." It was like being on a very uncomfortable blind date. Doubled. Way worse than facing into a wall of water in the middle of the ocean. His shoulders tightened and he concentrated on loosening them. He could do this. Annie was counting on him to do her job for her, and he was damned if he would let her down. Sweat prickled on his brow. He plastered a smile on his face, and prayed for Niall to help him out.

The tall redhead put him out of his misery. "I'm Sinead," she announced. "And this is Carol."

"What'll you have ladies?" Niall took their orders, and then gave Jack a surreptitious wink, as though he knew full well the agony Jack was suffering. "I'll bring them over."

Feeling as though he'd received a reprieve from execution, Jack pulled in a deep breath and dived in. "Come on over."

They followed him to the matchmaker's booth, where he set the book and camera down on the table. He shrugged off his jacket, and slung it over the back of his chair. The girls sat down opposite him. He swallowed, forcing down an unaccustomed flutter of butterflies.

"So, you're American?" Sinead eyed him suspiciously, as if he hailed from another planet, rather than another country.

"Yes, I'm a friend of Annie's. She asked me to help out." He plastered on his most reassuring and capable expression. "Annie's father is the regular matchmaker, and he'll be here tomorrow. I'm helping out for today. The process is pretty straightforward, let me take you through it."

Drinks flowed, and after a while, both girls let down their guard and honestly revealed what they were hoping for in a partner. Jack concentrated on the job at hand carefully writing down details. He even relaxed enough to get the shyer Carol talking.

When he coaxed a smile from her, he felt like he'd climbed Everest and stood, triumphant, at the summit.

"I'd really like to go on a date with someone good looking and fun, like you," Sinead teased. "What are you doing tonight?"

"Jack's Annie's boyfriend," Niall threw over his shoulder as he passed on his way back behind the bar. "He's taken."

Jack nodded. "I have plenty of wonderful men in here." He gripped the book tightly, as if to keep them from escaping. "I'm pretty sure I can sort you both out. Let's go outside and I'll take your pictures in the sun."

The bright sunshine was a shock after the dimness of the bar. He busied himself taking photographs of the smiling women, while his mind raced.

When Niall had declared he was taken, a peal of satisfaction reverberated to his core. In his other relationships, he'd always remained one step emotionally removed. Even when he thought he was in love, he held a part of himself back, unwilling to trust. He'd never craved belonging before, but with Annie it was different. His lungs expanded with clear sea air. Niall was right. He was taken.

ANNIE STRAIGHTENED and tossed the empty piping bag into the bin. She stretched her arms up and rotated tired shoulders. Her spine cracked, and she sighed aloud. *Only two more to go, then I'm finished.* A pristine white box awaiting her chocolates was on the counter. She shook her hands out, flexing cramped fingers. The silence in the kitchen set her nerves on edge. She flicked on the radio and tension flowed out of her body like water as classical music swelled in the empty room.

The last perfect crystallized violet she had spent ages preparing lay ready on a plate. It would take a steady hand to attach it perfectly. A nearby plateful of rejects bore testament to that. A bead of moisture trickled down her spine, as she inhaled the scent of warm chocolate. She aimed her 'point and click' thermometer at the heated vat and pulled the trigger.

The temperature was perfect. For the umpteenth time that day, she packed a pristine bag half-full, twisting the end so she'd have control over the contents. Next, she snipped the end with her scissors, bent from the waist, and carefully squeezed a shining pearl onto the chocolate's glossy surface. With the tweezers, she stuck down a perfect violet.

She peered at her plateful of entries, searching

for flaws. There weren't any. A wave of satisfaction rolled over her. They were *perfect*.

After the intensity of chocolate making, Annie yearned for a shower. Her upper arms ached with the strain of holding the same pose for hours. A massage would be heaven right now. At the mere thought of Jack's masterful hands working out her body's kinks she almost groaned aloud. She'd relived their conversation in the car all day. Obsessing over the moment his eyes had darkened to navy with desire as he kissed her. Jack's kisses had burned her up from the inside, melting her resolve to guard her heart. He was upfront and honest about what he wanted. He didn't promise forever like Steve had done.

She stripped off her clothes and climbed into the shower. Loading her sponge with lavender shower gel, she ran the bubbles over her body. The slightly abrasive surface of the sponge was deliciously arousing. She closed her eyes, let her head fall back, and imagined his calloused hands running over her breasts instead of the warm sponge. The blistering heat of their attraction was inescapable. Lovemaking with him would be spectacular; she just knew it. She turned up the heat, breathing in the lavender laden steam. He'd explained why he'd turned away from her on the beach, and she was ready to give him another try. It was time to take a chance on love.

EIGHT

Dinner with Bull, their plates on their knees in the sitting room, was an awkward affair without the distracting presence of the women to break the tension.

"You're a natural. You've a real flair for it." Bull finished his last mouthful of chicken pie, and edged the tray onto the sofa next to him. The moment Jack had returned from the pub, they'd worked through the book, discussing new people and outlining potential matches. It had been a long, hard process. One that continued over dinner. "You're good with people. You listen to them."

"It's what I do in my business." Warmth flooded Jack at Bull's approval. "In advertising it's important to find out what people really need."

"That's the way it is with matchmaking too," Bull's brow creased in a frown. "I'm not sure Annie understands that. It's not natural for her, never has been."

So at least Bull understood how difficult this was for Annie. That was a start. Maybe there was an alternative, one that didn't involve shoehorning her into a role she didn't want. He'd promised not to tell Bull her innermost thoughts, but he hadn't promised not to look for alternatives. Maybe in this time alone with Bull he could figure out something.

It was one thing to stand in as matchmaker for a day, but quite another to assume the mantle full time. Especially when you had another path in life. Annie's desire to succeed in her career consumed her. It was difficult to see how she could do both and be happy. She wasn't a natural matchmaker, but she was trying her best with the role heredity had dropped in her lap. Bull should give her a break.

"It's all to do with what people want. Her focus is to find them partners for life. Some want that, but not all of them. Some just want a sympathetic ear to listen. Others want to practice their pitch before trying it out on a date. The one thing they all have in common is they want a connection, a respite from loneliness. So many people are isolated and alone, Jack."

Bull's words sat like heavy lead in Jack's heart. Since the accident he'd wanted more than anything not to be alone, to be part of a family. In his long isolation, he'd almost given up hope of things ever being different.

"I know, Bull."

"Yes, you do." Bull patted his hand with his large paw. "That's what makes you a good matchmaker, Son. You recognize the need in others."

At a loss for words, Jack fell back on his standard response when things got too intense. Retreat. "I'll take the plates through. Would you like some coffee?" He gathered up their plates and pushed the door open. Gales of female laughter wafted through from the kitchen.

"And pie, but watch yourself in there," Bull warned. "The ladies can be dangerous."

"Evening, ladies."

A hush fell over the room. Glasses of Baileys Cream Liqueur and thick slabs of fruitcake balanced mid-way from table to mouth froze in the air as Jack was subjected to a thorough inspection.

"Jack. Pull a chair up and come sit," Maeve invited. The smell of warm apple pie filled the room, his mouth watered.

"I said I'd bring Bull some coffee, and some apple pie." He realized too late he'd walked himself into a situation it would be nigh on impossible to escape from.

"I'll get him some. You come and sit down here." Maeve patted the chair next to her. "My friends are dying to meet you."

A couple of drinks later, introductions made, Jack wondered what on earth Bull and Annie had warned him about. He was having more fun than he'd had in years.

"I must admit, Jack," Eileen confided. "You're not what I expected at all."

"No, you're not what I expected either." Mags helped herself liberally from the sherry bottle in the center of the table.

"I heard you were sort of rough and hairy— no offense." Eileen's eyes darted to his. "And a bit, sort of, y'know, well…"

"Manky, was the word I heard," Mags announced. She covered her mouth with her hand, as if realizing she'd gone a bit far. Even for her. "Not you, you understand, but your clothes." She patted Jack's arm.

"I had a makeover." Jack batted his eyelashes at them. A wave of giggles filled the room.

"For Annie?" Mags batted hers back, her voice laced with innuendo.

"For business," he replied. "I've a meeting on Monday in Dublin. To be honest, after spending weeks at sea I needed it."

"I'm glad." Eileen blushed. "I didn't see you before, but I think you're only gorgeous now."

Jack leaned over and kissed Eileen on the cheek. "Unfortunately, I'm taken." He grinned. The older woman blushed right to her white roots.

"Oh, you're a charmer, you are," she said. "I'd say you could talk the birds right down out of the trees."

"Just got to do the best I can with what I've got." The table erupted in laughter, and Jack helped himself to a slice of cake. *If you can't beat 'em join 'em.*

"So, how long are you in the country for?" Eileen asked. The sudden silence was so profound you could hear a pin drop. Jack chewed and swallowed. He shifted uncomfortably on the hard wooden chair. The open, curious faces focusing his direction pinned him to the spot.

"Well, I've some business…"

"In Dublin. On Monday," Eileen added.

"And someone I've got to find." They waited. "My grandmother." It was his most closely guarded secret, and they'd effortlessly winkled it out of him, like a snail from a shell.

"I didn't know you had a grandmother here," said Maeve. "Whereabouts in the country is she?"

"She lives in Greystones, on the coast, outside Dublin. I'm meeting her tomorrow for the first time."

Their friendly smiles transformed to concerned stares.

"I've never met her. I grew up in care."

The words wouldn't stop coming. For the first time in his life, warmth and support dissolved his barriers.

"She's one of the reasons I came to Ireland. I haven't talked about her before."

Maeve placed a glass of Baileys in front of him soundlessly, and he sipped it gratefully. The smooth chocolate cream warmed him with a welcome kick of whiskey. The silence was oppressive, stifling. Eileen walked around the table and put both her small hands on his shoulders, squeezing reassuringly.

"Thanks for telling us, Jack." The others murmured their agreement. "You're a good man; she'll love you." She patted his back before making her way back to her chair. In the silence of the room, a mobile phone rang.

Jack pulled the phone from his pocket. He glanced at the display before flicking it open. "Excuse me, ladies." He stood quickly and pushed the back door open. Alone in the darkness, he strode to the chair under the apple blossom.

"Did you say ladies?" Annie sounded incredulous. "You didn't go in there?"

"I went in there," he admitted, "and ended up telling them my whole godamned life story."

"Well, I warned you." He could hear a smile. She must be smiling. "Anything I should know about?"

"I think you were wrong, at least two of them are my type."

"Oh, funny. I've lost you then, have I?"

"No." It wasn't possible to joke with her anymore. Not when he ached to have her here, next to him. If she were he could wrap his arms around her and tell her how much she meant to him. Let her warmth and humor bolster him for tomorrow's showdown.

"So, did they prise any secrets out of you?"

"Yes." he stated flatly. "Something I haven't told anyone, not even you."

"What is it? What's wrong?"

His heart pounded in the silent darkness. "I came to Ireland to find my grandmother. I hired a private detective to trace her."

"Oh." The sound was tinged with shock.

"My parents died when I was eight. I remember it as if it were yesterday. There was a car crash and the car flipped over. After the paramedics cut me out, I sat on the back step of the ambulance. Watching them fight to save them."

The burning in his chest rose up into his throat, choking off the words. Tears prickled behind his eyes. It was the first time he'd talked of his parent's deaths. The first time he'd revealed his devastating grief since the day in the ambulance. Since that day he hadn't cried. There wasn't anyone to cry with.

"I knew when they stopped their frantic attempts my parents were dead. My life was shattered into pieces. Things would never be the same."

"Were there relatives, or friends?" Her voice trailed off in the darkness.

"My father worked on building sites. We moved every six months so they had no friends who could help. There wasn't anyone. At least, I didn't think so. Until I reached eighteen I didn't know there was anyone in the world with my DNA."

"That must have been terrible for you." Her empathy reached out to him through the long miles separating them. Her caring words a balm on his bruised soul. He hadn't revealed his torment to anyone in the long years since their deaths. Somehow talking to Annie changed everything. It still ached, but he didn't feel so alone.

There was a crack in his armor, an echo of the child he'd once been. The child who'd stared at unfamiliar ceilings wondering why there was no one who cared what happened to him. He shook it off, desperate to return to normality before he lost it altogether.

"Why didn't you come to find her before?"

"Long story." Not something to talk about over the phone. He needed to see and hold her. Explain how his grandmother refused to take in her grandchild. With no options, the authorities consigned him to the care system. He rubbed his hand over his knees, and changed the subject. " Have you made your chocolates?"

"Yes."

He breathed out in relief to be back on solid ground rather than the shifting sands of his childhood.

"After a lot of hard work I finally got them done." She described the intricate process she'd gone through during the day. How she'd made twenty-five chocolates, and ended up with only ten good enough. "To match a boxful, with the flowers all looking perfect…" She sounded tired. "Well, let's just say it was a lot more work than I'd expected."

"Did you leave some for me for tomorrow night?" he asked.

"Nope. Ate them all," she said.

"Well in that case, I'll have to think of something else we can have for dessert." At his provocative words, he heard a swift intake of breath. A wave of lust swept over him. She was feeling the attraction between them too.

"Well, I do have some chocolate left over. I guess I could blend it with some cream, so if you brought a paintbrush…"

"Body paint?" His heart stuttered and almost stopped.

"Are you any good at painting?" Her deep warm tones aroused him instantly.

"I've never tried, but I'm willing to take lessons." Painting it on and then licking it off. It was a process that could take hours. Long, delicious hours.

"Where are you?" Her voice was so clear in the darkness for a moment he could almost imagine she was sitting next to him.

"Sitting in the dark in the back garden. You?"

"In bed." Her voice dropped an octave. "Feeling lonely."

Jack moaned. His rampant imagination pictured her sitting up in bed. With mussed hair flowing over the soft skin of her shoulders. "You heard me, right? You understand I'm sitting in your parents back garden, on LADIES NIGHT, with the kitchen full of drunk women with x-ray vision." His voice dropped to match hers.

"With your voice whispering in my ear, and my whole body rioting at the thought of lying there next to you."

"I wish you were upstairs." Her voice was husky, aroused. "I'd like to tell you about what I'm wearing."

"Stop." He strode to the gate, unable to bear this particular brand of torture any longer. He needed to cool things down. "I've got an image to maintain here." He aimed for teasing, but missed it by a mile. "I'm supposed to be Jack Miller, the calm, reliable boyfriend of Annie Devine. Responsible matchmaker of this parish. I can't possibly be found wandering in the dark, muttering obscenities."

"For the sake of propriety I'd better say goodnight, then."

"When I see you tomorrow will you stay with me in my hotel? After dinner?"

"Try stopping me." Her husky whisper fanned the flames into blazing life again.

"Till tomorrow then." He returned to the chair under the tree. Breathed in the scent of Apple Blossom, heady and intensified by the night. Aroused, like never before, by the lingering echo of her voice.

I've got it bad. It was going to take a while sitting out here to cool his fevered body from the effect five minutes listening to Annie's husky voice had wrought.

Tires crunched to a stop on the gravel. A door slammed. The dark form of a lumbering giant carrying a large box struggled to open the gate. He stood up.

"Can I help?"

"Jaysus! What the hell are you doing in the dark?" The box slipped from the shrieking stranger's grasp and he stumbled.

Jack grabbed the box just in time. "Sorry, Mate, I didn't mean to startle you. Here, let me carry this in for you." He pushed the door open. His eyes scanned the room for a convenient place to stow the heavy box. Maeve swept a pile of newspapers off a table. He gratefully put it down.

"Michael! I see you've met Jack." Maeve nodded his direction.

"Not really," Michael said.

"Jack Miller." Jack reached for the outstretched hand and instantly regretted it. The man didn't know his own strength. Jack was pretty sure he heard the small bones in his hand cracking as they were painfully crushed.

"Ah! So you're Jack Miller, the boyfriend." Eyebrows raised theatrically. "Well, you're the man I'm looking for, so."

Jack eyed Michael cautiously. This didn't sound good.

"I'm Michael Devine, Sean's son," he explained. "He sent me down with the things for the boat."

Jack sighed out a breath. Relief flooded over

him. He'd feared Michael might be one of Annie's disgruntled suitors on the warpath. He grinned. "That's great." He peered into the box.

"He got everything you were looking for." Michael pulled out a list. "And he said to tell you he'll come down next week and help you fit everything."

"That's very kind of him, but…"

"Ah now, there's no need for but," Michael said sternly. "Since you arrived my father has spent his time staring out of his window at your boat. He's dying to get on board and poke around. He's always wanted a 'Bateau Rouge.' He keeps muttering: 'It's what dreams are made of.'"

"I like it." The one thing missing from his presentation was the perfect tagline. Out of the blue, Sean Devine had provided it for him.

"I'm away for a couple of days, but when I'm back I'll call in to him. I could do with a hand."

"Right, I'll tell him."

"Michael, Bull's in the sitting room. Why don't you go in for a visit?"

"Sounds good to me, Maeve." Michael snagged a bottle of whiskey and two glasses off the center of the table and made for the door. "Are you coming, Jack?"

"Sure."

Maeve handed him a glass from the cupboard.

"Nice meeting you, ladies." He slipped

through the door into the sitting room, in hot pursuit of the other men of the house.

Jack was 6 foot 4, so it was rare to find a taller man, but Michael topped him by a good two inches, and had shoulders that barely made it through the door. In deference to his size, Jack let him settle on the only armchair, and squeezed onto the sofa next to Bull, picking up the matchmaking book and balancing it on his knee.

"So, how's the matchmaking going?" Michael's bulk filled every inch of the chair, he stretched his legs out in an attempt at comfort.

"Grand. Jack's been helping, because Annie had to go to Dublin to make chocolates," Bull answered through a mouthful of pie. "She's got through to the finals."

"That's great." Michael shifted, pouring three mammoth whiskeys, and handing one to Jack. His graying hair was cut short, and stood up straight on his head, the rough bristles like a yard brush. "So, have either of ye made any matches?"

"Not me." Jack swirled the whiskey around in his mouth. The potent aroma assailing his nostrils, and permeating every pore. "I only stood in for today. There's potential though."

"I saw Noel out with a quiet one, they seemed to be getting on well." Michael seemed genuinely interested.

"Pass Michael the book, Jack. He knows the

locals, and might be interested to see whom we've matched with whom. Maybe you might come down and help me tomorrow, Michael?"

"I'd love to."

Jack handed the book into Michael's huge paw. Yes, Michael certainly was interested. He read through the details, making pertinent suggestions they hadn't considered. He was insightful, and focused. Why hadn't Bull asked Michael to step in when Annie was called away?

"So, Michael. Are you interested in matchmaking?" It wasn't his place to ask, but he asked anyway. There was silence for a moment. Bull put his empty plate onto the table, and picked up his whiskey.

"I am. It's in my blood I suppose. My grandfather was the matchmaker."

Bull swallowed a mouthful and spluttered. "Jaysus, that's strong." He grinned. "Michael always sat next to me when he was a kid. Soaking in the atmosphere and learning the craft. His father wasn't interested, so it fell to me to be the next matchmaker."

"After you, it'll be Annie." Michael's eyes dulled, disappointment evident in the way his mouth drooped at the corners.

Jack pulled in a deep breath. Annie didn't want it, and Michael so obviously did. She'd told him to keep her secret safe, but this was the perfect moment to pass the baton. If she were here, she'd speak. Tell them that she didn't want to be the next matchmaker. He didn't have an option; he needed to do this for Annie.

"Does it have to be Annie?"

There was silence as both men stared at him.

Indecision flickered across Bull's face, as if he'd never even considered the possibility she might not assume her inherited right.

"It's her inheritance. She's always known it's there for her." Bull set his mouth in a grim line. He crossed his arms and stared Jack down.

"You said yourself she's not a natural matchmaker. Are you sure she wants it?" He was venturing out onto a branch, and hoped to hell no one was going to cut it off. He couldn't reveal what he knew to be the truth; that would be betraying her confidence. But he could sow the seeds of doubt. Maybe if Bull saw he had options, he might talk to Annie about it, find out the truth from her lips, not Jacks.

Bull's face softened. "We've never spoken about it. I just presumed she wanted it."

Jack swallowed the last inch of whiskey in his glass. "Maybe you should ask her."

NINE

Jack ran a finger inside the collar of his new white shirt. The tight cotton chafed his neck, after so many weeks of tee-shirts. He fiddled with the blue striped tie, making sure it was straight, and undid his suit jacket. It was time. He breathed in a lungful of calming air, and pushed open the heavy glass door of the nursing home.

The smell assailed his nostrils. Disinfectant, cabbage and that indefinable old person smell. The grey paint of the lobby was thick and glossy. Doubtless easy to wash. The thought made his heart sink. Through an open door he glimpsed the dining room. Plates clattered, the sound of conversation swelled in the plain, serviceable room. His feet squeaked on shiny linoleum. It was lunchtime. Six elderly women and one old man sat around tables, while nurse's aids brought their meals. Jack sniffed. *Yes, definitely cabbage.* He couldn't see what else formed today's lunch, but whatever it was it didn't smell very appetizing. One of these women was his grandmother.

A nurse appeared at his side. "Can I help you?"

"I'm here to see Mary Byrne."

"Oh." A look of surprise flickered across her face. "You'd better come into the office." She maneuvered her trouser-clad ample bottom behind the desk, and gestured to the chair in front of her. "Please, take a pew." She smiled. "Are you a relative?"

"Her grandson." Anger tightened his chest and he clenched his hands into fists.

The woman pulled out a file from the filing cabinet just within reach. "I didn't know Mary had any family."

"My name is Jack Miller. My mother was her daughter. Can I see her?"

She tapped her pen on the file in front of her and avoided his eyes. "When was the last time you saw Mary?"

"Never," he ground out. "I've only just discovered she's still alive."

"You'll need to talk to the doctor first. I'll call him."

She bustled out. Jack cast an eye around the

tiny room, resisting the urge to swivel the file with his grandmother's name printed on the front. The tension rose to fever pitch, shredding what was left of his nerves. He glanced down at his white clenched hands, and made a conscious decision to relax them. The nurse had been nervous of him. Probably because he hadn't smiled. He relaxed his jaw, and tilted his head from side to side. He'd do better with the doctor.

The nurse came back and hovered in the doorway, allowing the doctor to precede her into the room. He was tall and thin, like an undertaker in a horror film. His wiry white hair formed an irregular halo. He shooed the nurse away and took her seat.

"Mr. Miller. I'm Dr. Lynch. Good to meet you." His Adams apple bobbed up and down and he swallowed. He fidgeted for a moment and avoided Jack's eyes. Eventually he pulled himself together. His hands stilled on the file in front of him, as he echoed the nurse's words.

"We didn't know Mary had any relatives. Nobody's visited her since her husband died."

"I didn't know Mary was still alive. I've been living in America. I came the moment I found her." Jack didn't want to waste time going over the old story. He'd waited long enough for this moment. But there were protocols to follow. He forced a tight smile.

"I'm sorry to tell you, Mr. Miller, but your grandmother has severe Alzheimer's." The older man's face was full of sympathy. "I'm afraid she won't remember you."

He'd come all this way for nothing. Jack stared at the swirly patterns on the worn linoleum, and gathered a response. "I've never met her." Emptiness opened up a chasm in his chest. Now he'd never know why she abandoned him. "My mother was pregnant when my parents eloped. She cut all links with her family because they didn't approve of my father. I was born in America. They never looked back and I never knew of my roots. When they died in a car crash, the authorities wrote to Mary and asked her to adopt me. She refused."

The doctor flicked through the file open in front of him. "How old were you?"

"I was just a child. I ended up in the care system." There was no need to go into further detail, as a doctor working within the health service; no doubt Dr. Lynch could imagine what that was like.

"Mary came to us ten years ago from Dundrum Mental Hospital." He read through the yellowing documents. Pieced together his patient's history. "According to this she was admitted in nineteen seventy-eight. She had serious mental problems which necessitated long term hospitalization."

"My parents died in nineteen eighty." Three years after she was committed.

"There's a letter here." The doctor turned a piece of paper around and slid it across the desk. Jack read it. The letter was addressed to Mary and said she had an orphaned grandchild. A grandson who needed her help.

"Did she ever see it?" His pain and anger were dissolving, like an iceberg in salty water.

The doctor flicked through pages, and stopped when he found what he was searching for. "This is the report." He tapped his yellowing teeth with a fingernail. His glasses slipped forward and he pushed them back up with a finger. "On receipt of the letter detailing the sudden death of her only child, we have today had a policy meeting to determine our response. Mary Byrne's medical condition is permanent with no possibility of recovery." He looked up. "They go into more detail of her condition. I'll skip over it."

Jack nodded, he didn't need the details.

"In conclusion, it's decided she will never be able to offer a home to her grandchild. Breaking the news of her daughter and son-in-law's death has resulted in another episode. We have written to the American authorities and asked them to place the child for adoption for there can be no home provided for him by our patient."

Adoption would have been preferable to his foster homes. But no one wanted to adopt a troubled eight-year old. Not when there were babies available. Taking on a child would be too much for almost anyone.

"Does she know I exist?" Sadness descended like freezing fog. The chill went so deep his heart froze. He wished Annie were with him. Facing this alone was much worse than he'd imagined.

"I'm sorry, Mr. Miller, I'm afraid she doesn't. She's too far gone now to understand."

"I'd like to meet her." The anger was gone, replaced by a lingering sadness that she'd never be able to give him the family that he so desperately wanted. But she was alone too. They needed each other, even if she had no idea that her blood flowed in his veins.

The doctor's eyes searched his. "You realize she won't be able to understand who you are?"

"Yes." Pity for the woman he'd been ready to hate flooded him. "But I'm still her family. At least one of us knows that."

It was a plain room with few possessions. A bookshelf held an old bible and a few well-thumbed paperbacks. It smelt of disinfectant mixed with something sweeter. He spotted a bottle of perfume on the table. *Lily of the valley*. One of his mother's favorites too. An old woman, propped up on a mountain of cushions, lay in bed. Her white hair was carefully styled; she was wearing a warm pink bed jacket. Faint traces of face powder clung to her cheeks, and she had lipstick on. She looked well cared for, and happy.

"Mary, I've brought someone to see you." The doctor smiled, and she smiled back. "This is Jack. He's come from America."

"My husband is called Jack." She had his mother's eyes.

She waved in the direction of a small table cluttered with framed photographs. He wandered over. The first picture he saw was one of his mother. White noise rushed into his ears and tears pricked his eyes. He hadn't seen the picture before, but he'd know her anywhere. She was in her teens in the photograph but she looked just like she did in his memory. A tiny vase containing sweet Williams sat carefully on a small linen circle surrounded in lace. It was a shrine. Each framed picture was free of dust, although the rest of the room looked less well tended to. It was a shrine to his mother's memory.

He picked up a photo of a family group. It was Mary, her husband and his mother. He handed it to her.

"Tell me about them."

TEN

Jack climbed the steps of the townhouse, and pressed the bell.

"Hello?" Annie's disembodied voice drifted from the intercom.

"It's me." He waited for the buzz of the automatic door, but nothing happened. Instead, he heard her breathless voice again.

"I'll be down in a minute."

He walked back to the car and looked up. Wondering which flat was hers. The netted curtains gave no hint. His eyes flickered to the front door again. How much longer was she going to be? Urgency and anticipation cut a hole in his gut. He needed her. Standing out here waiting was torture. The door slammed.

Annie stood on the doorstep. A muted silver

dress clung to every curve. Her hair flowed around her shoulders, the ends hidden by the pink shawl fastened just above her breasts with a silver broach. His heart thudded hard in his chest. She sashayed down the steps toward him.

"You look amazing," he managed to croak out when she stood in front of him.

"So do you." She looked him up and down with a stunned expression. "You look different."

He wrapped his arms around her and pulled her close, kissing her hard. Her bag slipped from her grasp to the ground. She wrapped her arms around his waist and responded.

Her fragrance, a soft blend of flowers and lemon teased his senses, and time and place faded away. His palms stroked her back through the silky silver of her dress. The last thing he wanted was dinner. He was sorely tempted to carry her inside her apartment and peel the silver sheath off her.

She pulled back slightly, and he noted with satisfaction her uneven breathing. "I brought some clothes with me, for tomorrow," she said.

Jack loosened his grip and leant back on the car. She bent to retrieve her bag, showcasing a long stretch of perfect leg. Satisfaction welled up in him. "Good. Did you bring the body paint too?" His voice was light and teasing, and her skin pinkened with a blush.

"I thought I'd save that for our second date."

Her dimple flashed. He felt a rush of relief. After the day he'd had he didn't think he'd be calm enough to carefully paint her. It would take too much time.

"You better not lean against this car, the owner won't like it." She straightened, the bag clenched tightly in her hand.

"I don't mind it one bit." He took her bag from nerveless fingers. "I'll put the bag in the back. Climb in."

———

THE BEIGE LEATHER was warm against her bare legs, the walnut dash gleamed as little glints of light from the city's streetlights bounced off it. Annie trailed a hand over the upholstery, nostrils flaring at the scent of warm leather mixed with Jack's cologne. She glanced sideways at him as the car pulled away from the curb. He looked different. His haircut revealed the sharp angles to his face, making him look stronger, more powerful somehow. And the clothes were a revelation. The black shirt clung to his shoulders, making her painfully aware of their breadth. When she'd come out of the apartment and walked towards him she'd scanned him head to toe, and she liked what she saw.

"I thought we could eat in the hotel." The big

car wove deftly through the traffic. He flicked the indicator and pulled into an underground car park.

Jack walked around to open her door, and slid his arm possessively through hers. They climbed into the lift, sexual tension sparking the inches between their bodies as the numbers counted upward. Her nostrils flared with the familiar scent of his cologne. She felt his body heat as he stood silently next to her, and itched to be closer. She wanted to reach for his hand, to make physical contact, but if she did she'd be in his arms tearing his clothes off frantically in mere moments. Half naked and sweaty wouldn't be the way to arrive in the lobby. She clenched her hands at her sides, to avoid acting on her impulses.

The door slid slowly open into a plush corridor with rooms leading from it. Presumably, they were going to the room to drop off her overnight case before dinner. She followed him down the corridor, heels sinking in the thick carpet. He opened a door into an elegant suite.

Sumptuous pelmeted curtains of a rich dark gold softened long glass windows facing Dublin's inner city park, St Stephen's Green. A glittering chandelier hung from the ceiling. Below it was a large dining table, set for two with silver cutlery and crystal glasses.

"It seemed a shame not to use the dining

table." He unfastened the broach at the front of her dress, and removed her shawl with gentle fingers. "I didn't want to be in a room full of people tonight."

"We're eating here?" Her heart fluttered like a captive bird longing to break free and fly out of the cage of her ribs. She glanced at him, and bit her lip. For the first time, her stomach clenched as she registered the changes in him. Last night, after their hot flirtation on the phone, she'd dreamed of them together. His hair was long, and she'd peeled his worn tee-shirt over his head to stroke over his hard chest as he stripped her of her negligee and ran his scorching lips all over her body. Now, she was alone in the hotel room of a man she barely recognized. It wasn't just the shorter hair. The strong line of his jaw made him different somehow. Harder. She glanced down at his grey suit, insecurity gnawing at her. It was a very expensive grey suit. To match his very expensive car.

"Yes. We're eating here." Oblivious to the emotions warring within her, he strode to the telephone and called room service. "They'll be up with dinner in a few minutes." He plucked a bottle of champagne from a waiting ice bucket and filled two glasses. "Here, have something to drink."

"This must have cost a lot of money. What did you do, rob a bank?" she joked to cover her unease. She felt awkward, unsure. This polished stranger offering her a glass of champagne didn't seem like the same man she'd known in Durna.

"What's the matter?" He stepped closer, and she stepped back, away from him.

Betrayal and confusion warred within her. The old, easygoing, longhaired Jack was gone. The Jack she'd been falling in love with. Echoes of his ghost lingered, but her heart plummeted. When Steve left her at the altar she'd found out she was useless at judging someone's character. His actions had brutally proved that. Had she made the same mistake again? The distance between them was more than just physical. It was mental.

"I thought I knew you, but now I'm here," she flung her arm around the sumptuous suite, "in a suite which must cost more than two month's rent of my flat, I don't know that I do."

She swept him foot to toe with a glance. "It's not just the hair, the clothes, and the car. You're different." Her chest constricted. She reached out and laid the palm of her hand flat on his chest, unable to stop herself from touching him. "I guess I'm confused. Because I feel like there's so much about you I thought I knew, but now realize I don't." She pulled her hand back. Her emotions tangled into a knot, so open and vulnerable it almost hurt.

"I'm still me." He ran a hand over her hair.

"I'm still the man you decided to spend the night with." Tension grew between them like the moment before the curtain pulls back on opening night. He was going to kiss her. Her tongue quickly darted over tingling lips and her eyes drifted close. She heard a swift intake of breath. The hand caressing her disappeared. She opened her eyes in confusion.

"We'll eat, and talk, and get to know each other better." He stepped away.

"I've had a hell of a day." He ran his hand through his hair. The shorter strands stood up in a familiar way. Reassuringly like the old Jack.

A DISCREET KNOCK HERALDED the arrival of their dinner. Jack opened the door and a waiter quickly wheeled a trolley inside. "I've set the appetizers out, Sir." He left the remainder under domed silver covers.

"Thank you." Jack slipped him a bill, and walked him to the door. "We'll leave the trolley outside when we're finished."

"Certainly, Sir."

They were alone again. The difference in his appearance and the evidence of his wealth had shocked Annie. For some reason she was pulling away from him. It wasn't a situation he was prepared to tolerate. He burned to kiss her, and to peel the dress off her enticing body, but battled down his urges. Everything about their first night together had to be perfect. It was worth taking the time to reassure her that although the wrapping was different, he was the same as he'd ever been.

"I ordered for us, I hope you like crab?" Jack pulled out a chair for her.

"I love it." She eyed the cocktail of crabmeat, lettuce, watercress and glossy mayonnaise greedily. "I'm starving!"

"I had an eventful day. Today I did something I'd dreamed of for years."

"Drove a kick-ass car?" Good. She was joking again. He rubbed the back of his neck. After the emotional overload of meeting Mary he didn't know how much more emotion he could take.

"No, I drive a kick-ass car at home. This car is definitely a step down from my Aston Martin." He smiled at her expression. She really looked cute with her mouth slightly open, even though she probably wouldn't think so.

"You met your grandmother."

"Yes." He poked at the crabmeat, loaded a forkful and chewed. "After my parents died I grew up in a succession of foster homes." He clenched his fist on the tabletop. She reached across and placed her smaller hand on his. "It wasn't a happy experience. That's why I envy you your family. For years, I hoped some relative would come and claim me. I wanted a home like my school friends had. You know, a mother, father, maybe even some siblings. Yearned for it actually."

The crab salad was delicious, but he was too jaded to care. He forked another mouthful in, and chewed slowly. "But it wasn't to be. When my parents were alive they never talked about the past. I found out after they died, that they'd eloped from Ireland. When I got my advertising agency off the ground, and could afford it, I employed a private investigator to trace my ancestry. That's when I found Mary Byrne, my mother's mother."

"She never came for you?" Annie whispered.

"No. I thought about it constantly. I wondered what sort of a woman would leave her own blood to fend for himself, alone and orphaned, in another country. Today I found out."

He could tell she wanted to say something. The air was charged with her unasked questions and her gaze never wavered from his. She squeezed his hand briefly and waited.

"I drove past the house my mother grew up in. You can see the sea from there. For a moment, I imagined myself there as a child looking out at the sea across a garden full of flowers." His mouth tightened into a narrow line. "I'm long over it now, but my childhood was hard. I was always getting into fights. I can't remember the amount of times I sneaked inside the house with a bloody lip." As a small child he'd been vulnerable, growing up in the foster home. An easy target.

"So today when I went to meet my grandmother I was ready to hate her. I wanted to hurt her. I needed to prove her neglect and abandonment hadn't broken me." He poured them both another glass of champagne and swallowed his in one gulp. "Then I saw her, and she looked so like my mother…"

He swallowed. *Like my mother might look if she'd lived to get old. Not the way she looks in my memory. Warm, smiling with love for me, young.*

"What did she say?" Annie asked gently.

"She has Alzheimer's." A nerve in the corner of his jaw twitched. He pulled in a ragged breath. "She had no idea I even existed. She's never known. She had a mental illness, and her doctors never told her."

"Oh!" Annie covered her mouth with her hand, visibly distressed.

"My mother eloped when she was a pregnant teenager with a boy from the village. He asked my grandparents for her hand in marriage, but they refused. They said their daughter was too young. She was only seventeen."

"But the baby…"

"They kept the pregnancy a secret, and ran away. Mary told me her husband was waiting for his daughter to return and apologize. She thinks he's alive, most of the time. Her doctor told me my grandfather died shortly after my parent's ashes came back from the States. Mary's mental illness meant she was never told about the sole survivor."

"You," Annie said softly.

"Me." Jack nodded.

She slipped her hand into his, gripping it tightly. "What a day."

"She has my mother's pictures everywhere. If she could have given me a home she would have. I'm sure of it."

"Did you tell her you were her grandson?"

"No. Her doctor felt it would be too confusing. She wouldn't be able to understand. We talked for an hour before she fell asleep."

"What are you going to do?" Her soft hair fell forwards as she leaned in closer, lying in a shining coil against her clavicle.

"I'll visit her again before I go. Perhaps I can move her to America. Find a nursing home close by."

The pain of recounting the story faded with Annie's slow smile, and the tension holding his body in thrall released him.

"Are you ready for the main course?"

Annie nodded. He stood, and quickly swapped the plates from the trolley.

"Any more secrets?" she asked later when they'd finished their meal.

"Well, I'm rich."

"You sort of let that one out of the bag," she teased.

"And I'm not really a sailor."

"No kidding."

"I own my company. I've built it into one of the top advertising agencies in New York. I sailed to Ireland to put the yacht through its paces. I'm giving a presentation to the manufacturers, Bateau Rouge, tomorrow. My company is bidding for their global advertising campaign. In order to sell something successfully I need to have a real feel for its strengths and weaknesses. My approach is to live with the product and learn to love it. I know the yacht inside out. Apart from blue water, it was all I had to concentrate on for the weeks I spent at sea."

"So, that's why you sailed across the Atlantic?" Her fingers played with the napkin.

"I wanted to be alone to think about meeting my grandmother, too." Drained by the emotional baggage he'd managed to offload, Jack strove to lighten the mood. "Enough about me. I want to hear about you." He poured the coffee in a thin stream, and carried it to the table in front of the heavily upholstered old gold sofa.

She sank into its soft upholstery. Her dress slid up revealing more of her silky legs. "Gosh, this sofa's eating me whole."

He swallowed as a vivid image flashed unfettered through his mind. Annie and him. Nude.

"When will you hear about the Chocolate Oscar Competition?" They needed to talk. There would be time for touching later.

"Tonight's the judging. Tomorrow morning they'll make their final decision. I've given them my mobile number, so my future continues the moment the phone rings."

Jack stared. *Surely the competition couldn't mean so much to her?*

"I'm pretty sure your future's going to continue whether the phone rings or not."

He sat next to her, running a finger down her lightly tanned arm. A shiver of goosebumps signaled her response.

"Well, I mean, my future's going to continue the way I want it to. The way I've planned." She talked quickly the way she always did when she was trying to explain something. "If I win the competition I'll have my own premises. A fantastic chocolate shop, right in the center of Dublin. It's all I've ever wanted."

Heaviness settled in Jack's chest. She had her future mapped out. A future that didn't include him. He'd planned on suggesting she join him in New York. Took a little holiday to explore their relationship further. He wanted them to be together; hadn't reckoned on her having alternative plans.

"Why do you have to be here?"

She looked at him in astonishment.

"Not you too. You sound like my father."

"We spent a lot of the past twenty-four hours talking," he said. "Although, surprisingly, not all about you."

She pouted. "Huh," she tossed back her hair. "I've spent my life trying to escape the west of Ireland, and Dublin's my inspiration. The shop in Dublin is part of the prize, it's a wonderful opportunity. Even if I don't win, a big city is the ideal place for a chocolate shop; there wouldn't be the business in Durna to sustain it. As for Dublin? It's difficult to explain. I need to show you. What time is your presentation tomorrow?" She tilted her head sideways, gazing at him through half closed lids.

"Twelve-thirty."

"Plenty of time." She smiled enigmatically. "Now, Jack Miller, I think you promised me double helpings of dessert."

Her pupils expanded as he rose slowly to his

feet. She plucked at the hem of her dress, but her fingers stilled on the silvery material as he reached out a hand and pulled her up. Her lips parted slightly. Her skin looked so soft he had to touch it. Long, dark eyelashes fluttered shut at the touch of his fingers on her cheekbone. The time for talking was over. Soft lips parted under the pressure of his, and their tongues tangled in a sensuous dance. His mind went blank. Her hands slid around him in one smooth movement, holding him tight.

His lips trailed down the long length of her throat. He pushed her hair back roughly and his teeth nipped her clavicle. She shuddered, and gripped him tighter. His breathing quickened and her chest rose and fell in a frantic rhythm.

"You're driving me totally insane, do you know that?" The admission ground out of him at the look of naked desire in her eyes. Heat blazed through him like fire through a dry forest. He picked her up with one smooth movement. Strode into the bedroom. Placed her gently on the gold silk bedspread.

She reached for her shoes.

"Let me." His voice was so husky and deep he barely recognized it. With shaking hands he carefully undid the straps holding the sandals in place, and slipped her feet out. Her high arch quivered when he ran his finger over it.

"Jack." She squirmed, trying to pull him to her.

"Shhh." He stroked her foot again. The skin was like soft silk under his fingertips. "Let me unzip your dress." He reached around and slid the zip slowly down. The material glided off her shoulders to reveal breasts barely covered by the ivory lace of her bra. She shimmied and he tugged the silver sheath off in one smooth movement. Dressed only in ivory silk and lace panties and an expression of deep desire, her obvious need of him was the most arousing thing he'd ever seen.

"Come over here," she commanded. A long elegant arm reached for him, and his seduction plan dissolved. With eager fingers he peeled off his jacket and shirt, and then wrestled with the noose of a tie, which suddenly seemed impossible to rip off.

"JACK," she breathed. God, she'd thought he was sexy when he'd picked her up without a word and carried her into the bedroom. Now she was desperate to stroke her hands over the wide expanse of golden chest dusted with a smattering of black hair his struggle with his shirt had revealed. He was perfect. And she wanted him. With an urgency bordering on obsession.

The muscles of his stomach contracted as he undid his belt buckle. At the sight, her inner muscles tightened too. He stepped out of his trousers, freeing an impressive erection barely contained by his black briefs. Stormy ocean blue eyes never left hers.

The bed compressed under his weight, and his firm lips claimed hers in a punishing kiss. Waves of sensation broke over her as the silken warmth of his body brushed against hers in a totally delicious sensuous onslaught.

"I wish we could stay here for days. I can't think of anywhere I'd rather be than here with you." She felt his words against her mouth. There were darker flecks around his iris, like planets in his own personal solar system. Their eyelashes were scant centimeters apart. It was totally absorbing, like drowning in deep water. The sensation was more intimate than the near nakedness of their bodies.

"Me too."

Fingers brushed her shoulders, and trailed over the top of her breasts.

"It's a front opener." She muttered huskily. Clever fingers undid the hidden clasp. Slipped it off.

"You're so beautiful."

Her nipples stood to attention, desperate for his touch. They were not disappointed. He teased one erect bud between his fingers, while his warm mouth clamped over the other. Heat blazed, liquefying her core, and she gasped out loud.

He sucked. She couldn't stop her frantic fingers from gripping his neck, holding him close. His clever mouth moved to her other breast; his fingers feathered over her ribs. Moved over her stomach. She arched into him, desperate have him closer.

"These are very pretty panties." His mouth traced the lace border and his fingers stroked the damp satin between her legs. She couldn't speak. She was drowning in a sea of sensation. When his hot mouth covered the satin, her hips pushed towards him.

"Jack."

His fingers caught under the delicate wisp of fabric, pulling it off. He tossed it roughly aside and grinned up at her.

"Patience, Darling." His mouth returned to its languid meanderings. Deliberate hands eased her legs apart, his tongue found her swollen nub, teasing it until she could bear no more.

His soft hair brushed her sensitive inner thigh. "I want you. I want you *now*."

At the note of desperation in her voice, he

stopped what he was doing. Kissed slowly up her body again. Nuzzled her neck.

"I want you too," he whispered in her ear, taking her ear lobe into his mouth and nipping it.

His warm chest covered hers and he reached for the bedside drawer. With shaking fingers he pulled out a small foil packet, shucked off his briefs and quickly sheathed himself. His smooth hardness nudged her once, and then sank deep inside.

She sighed as her body adjusted to his length. His chest brushed against her sensitized nipples, goosebumps erupted over her entire body. It was like being on a roller coaster; emotions coming so hard and fast she could hardly breathe. Her inner muscles contracted at the sensation of his body moving slowly, deliberately inside her. Her fingers caressed the smooth flex of muscles across his back, her thumb wandering of its own volition to trace his ribs.

Mine. A possessive wave of sensation flowed into her when he gasped. *You're mine.* She closed her eyes loving the feel of him inside her.

"Open your eyes," he commanded. His eyes were deep navy pools, the expression in them so intense she could barely breathe. This was so much more than sex. *I love you.* The words hovered on her lips, but remained unspoken. She couldn't speak the words aloud, it would change everything forever and she knew he wasn't ready to hear them. An invisible, unbreakable thread bound her to him. She was in a world of trouble.

They hadn't spoken of love, this was just a fling, a fling they'd both agreed on. She'd changed the rules by falling in love with him.

He moved faster, withdrawing slightly and then filling her more completely. The delicious pressure of his body transcending anything she'd ever felt before.

"Annie." His deep tone reverberated through the hard tips of her nipples. Her fingers caressed his ribs, holding on for dear life. Her breath stuttered out in quick gasps, every inhalation breathing in his essence. Every cell reached out to him, the heady thrill building and building. She clenched her jaw. Her thighs trembled. His lips moved over her jaw line and her mouth instinctively turned toward his like a flower seeking the sun. Their tongues tangled frantically as the waves of orgasm flooded over her. Inner muscles contracting again and again as his big body followed hers over the edge into bliss.

Eventually, her breathing steadied, and her heart rate slowed to near normal. The weight of his body on top of her was delicious. She tilted her hips, and moved sinuously against him.

"I'm too heavy." He tried to push himself up away from her, but she held him in place.

"Stay where you are, I like it."

"You're a complete masochist," he teased. "I'm heavy, I must be squashing you."

"You are." She grinned. Loving the weight of him. "Nothing better." She wrapped her arms tightly about him, nipples tingling against his hard chest. "You can't tell me you're not enjoying this."

"I could try, but somehow I know you wouldn't believe me." He undulated slowly and she gasped as he grew within her again. "Yes," he answered her unspoken question. "I want you again, which is pretty spectacular, even for me."

"Sex god?"

"Apparently so. But I don't think the condom can take it." He carefully extricated himself. Climbed out of bed and walked toward the bathroom. "I'll be back in a moment."

She linked her arms behind her head shamelessly admiring every inch of his naked body until he disappeared from view. It was chilly on top of the blanket. On shaky legs, she slipped off the bed, pulled back the covers, and climbed in.

Her lips were swollen and tender, she probed them carefully with the tip of her tongue. Then she snuggled under the warm cloud of duvet. Stretched out her legs and pointed her toes under the covers.

The muted sound of running water trickled in from the bathroom.

Where do we go from here? Our lives are on opposite sides of the world. An unwelcome little voice nagged, but she pushed it away. She rolled onto her side, pulling her knees up to her chest to assume the fetal position. If she won the competition, she'd have a perfect start to her chosen career. The Dublin chocolate shop came complete with a fully stocked chocolatier's kitchen, and the competition organizers would pay a contribution toward the cost of employing an assistant. The deal was only for a year, but after that her business should be well enough established that she could move out and find a premises of her own. It was the chance of a lifetime. She'd spent long hours working on the figures, and by sharing the flat, had saved enough to cover her startup costs. It was her one chance at success. A success she'd dreamed about for years.

After sleeping with Jack, her mind had wandered into unfamiliar territory. She'd always wanted to travel, and errant visions of them living together in New York made her head ache. She rubbed her forehead, willing the pain away. This dalliance with Jack had started as a quick affair, but had quickly morphed into something else entirely.

I don't want to be on the opposite side of the world from Jack.

She slipped the flat of her hand under her face on the pillow, her other hand resting on her wrist. And jumped when the telephone rang loudly on the bedside table.

"Jack, phone!" He didn't hear her above the sound of the water, so she scooted up in bed, reaching for the receiver. "Hello?"

"Hi, is Jack there?" The American accented voice was hesitant, as though the caller thought maybe she'd got the wrong number. Obviously she wasn't expecting a woman in Jack's hotel suite.

"I'll just get him for you. Who's calling?" It was a reasonable question, but she wasn't fooling herself. She wasn't being efficient. She wanted to know the identity of the stranger on the other end of the phone.

"It's Roxie," the voice proclaimed confidently.

An arrow of jealousy skewered her. *Who the hell was Roxie?* She swallowed it down, forcing her 'efficient' voice. "Okay, just a moment please." She slipped out of bed, not bothering to cover her nakedness and pushed open the bathroom door. "Roxie's on the phone."

He grabbed two white robes from behind the door, and handed her one. He toweled his body quickly and put the other one on. "It's work," he kissed her neck. Strode to the phone. "Roxie, what's going on?"

He sat on the bed, his eyes rising heavenward at the sound of Roxie's voice leaking from the receiver. "No, Roxie, you don't know her. She's a friend, someone I met in Durna. Yes, during the matchmaking festival." He glanced at Annie apologetically. She climbed back into bed next to him, too fascinated by his conversation to do the decent thing and give him privacy.

"Look, Roxie, I'm sure you rang for a reason, not just to interrogate me about my private life." He was all business suddenly, the harsh edge to his voice letting the caller know he wasn't happy about her questioning. "No, I haven't seen your email." He listened for a moment, frowning. "I'll power up the laptop. Set up a conference call and call back in five minutes."

He hung up and turned to Annie. "I'm sorry, there's a problem at the office. I'm going to have to deal with it." He walked to the closet and pulled on a pair of jeans and an old sweatshirt. "Do you want a cup of tea or something?"

His smile didn't quite reach his eyes. His attention was completely focused elsewhere. The familiar Jack was gone; the man in front of her an efficient stranger.

"I'll make us some." She followed him into the

sitting room. Made her way to the corner unit where basic supplies were set up.

"Thanks." He opened his briefcase wide on the table and turned on his laptop. By all indications getting ready to settle in for a solid few hours work.

"I'm taking mine back to bed." She put the cup down next to him. Willing his eyes to look her direction, wanting him to kiss her softly before she left.

"Thanks." His eyes never left the screen.

The phone rang again as she walked away. She entered the sumptuous bedroom and closed the door. Weakness stole over her body and she slumped against it. She could just make out the deep murmur of his voice. How could he turn off so quickly? Her entire body was still rioting at his remembered caresses. She put her tea down on the bedside table, climbed into bed, and pulled the covers up to her nose.

What on earth had she gotten herself into?

ELEVEN

It wasn't every day a major client had a tantrum. In fact, Jack couldn't remember the last time it happened. Unfortunately, Mecredi Cars took an immediate and violent dislike to Mark's campaign and wouldn't be mollified.

They wanted Jack. He was the head of the company and the client's happiness was his responsibility. Talk about bad timing.

When Annie gave him the tea, he'd had to bite down on his lip to stop reaching for her. The slightest touch of her body would have been enough to divert him from his goal and he hadn't been able to risk it. Not with Roxie phoning back any minute. Now, Annie lay alone next door, and he longed to lie there with her. He wanted to whisper how much he still wanted her, cover her skin with his hands, and his lips. Watch her dimple dent her cheek as her body responded to his caresses. Instead, he had no option but to review all the storyboards and talk through a potential solution with his team. Jason Mecredi was waiting for his call.

The television had gone on in the bedroom hours before. He'd dragged himself away long enough to stick his head around the door for a moment between calls, and found Annie asleep. She lay diagonally across the bed, the sheet flung back to reveal acres of creamy leg.

He'd tucked the sheet around her, and stroked the glorious hair fanned out behind her sleeping face. He wanted to climb into bed with her and kiss her awake, press his naked body against hers. A wave of yearning tightened his body into painful awareness.

Business had always come first. It had been his driving force for years. Now, for the life of him, he wished he could leave it to someone else. That couldn't happen. The Mecredi Cars contract was too important. It wasn't just his livelihood on the line, it was his whole company's future that was at stake. People depended on him; he couldn't disappoint them. Tomorrow he had a busy day with Bateau Rouge; he wouldn't have time to deal with Mecredi Cars as well. He cursed under his breath, and crept out, closing the door softly behind him.

Alone in the sitting room again, the enormity of the task ahead was daunting. Mecredi Cars were being completely irrational and dictatorial, insisting that he present a new strategy to them in person. He pushed a hand through his hair, and called room service, ordering a pot of strong coffee. Forcing thoughts of Annie away, he started to work. It seemed impossible, but he had to block her out of his thoughts for a few hours. His company depended on it.

ANNIE WOKE with warm fingers stretched over the soft skin of her stomach. Firm thighs curved around hers. She could feel the deep regular expansion of Jack's chest against her back. She snuggled closer, unable to hold back a little satisfied moan. His arm tightened in response. He was definitely awake and obviously enjoying the sensation of holding her too. Morning whiskers nuzzled her neck and she wriggled in delight.

"What time is it?" Jack's voice was deliciously deep and sleepy. They hadn't pulled the curtains last night. Sunlight flowed into the room. Annie reached for her watch.

"Nine-thirty."

"Damn." With one smooth movement, his hand disappeared. He pulled himself up in the bed. She turned around, scooting up to rest her back against the headboard next to him.

"All I want to do is stay here, and make love to you again." He brushed his lips against hers briefly. "But today will be a hell of a day. We need to get some breakfast and get on with it." He grinned at her ruefully. "Not much of a night, was it? I'm sorry, honey."

"I thought last night was pretty spectacular, actually." She reached out to stroke his chin, his stubble rough against her fingertips. "Up until the phone call." She'd lain awake waiting for him until sleep finally triumphed. He must have crept into bed in the early hours.

"There's a problem with a client." He ran his hand through his hair.

He looks even better this morning. Her fingers trailed over his naked chest. *Why does bed-head look so delicious on a man?*

"I'm going to have to go back to the States sooner than expected."

Their time together was ending before it had really begun. She flattened her palm against his chest, feeling his heart beat steady and strong.

"What about your boat?" *What about us?* But there was no us, was there? Not really.

"I'm only going back for a few days. I have to

sort out a few things. I thought maybe you might come with me."

There were so many things to do. The matchmaking festival was only half way through, and there was the question of the Chocolate Oscars. If she won, there would be a presentation. It would be impossible to get away.

"The festival is on until the end of next week. There's a party at the end of it."

"We'd be back in time." He tilted her mouth up towards him, staring at her lips with a determined fascination. Her heartbeat thumped faster.

"I want you to come to the States with me. I need you to. Say you will." He kissed her so thoroughly she almost forgot the question.

"I don't know. There's the competition…"

"Oh yeah, the competition." He pulled back. "I forgot about the competition."

"Well, I can't," she said firmly. "I will find out today if I've won it, and if I have, there's the presentation…" Her voice trailed off. His eyes clouded. Even though his arm was stroking her absently, his mind was somewhere else. He must be thinking of New York.

"We'll talk about it later. Let's have a shower. I want to get down and get some breakfast."

"Have we time to go out for it? I want to take

you somewhere." She climbed out of bed, and dressed in the fluffy white robe.

"That depends." The devilish light was back in his eyes. He tugged her closer with the belt of her robe. "I need to make sure I've washed every inch of you, thoroughly."

He bit her neck gently then led her unresistingly in the direction of the shower, his wicked smile letting her know she would come out of the shower very, very clean.

Stephen's Green was abuzz with crowds of people, all of them going the opposite direction. Like minnows swimming through a determined school of fish, they meandered down Grafton Street. Annie clutched Jack's hand tightly.

"It's just down here." The street was closed to cars. Flower sellers had set up stands on the sidewalk. They avoided the colorful stands of flowers set out before the bustling crowds by the flower sellers who had a regular pitch on the street. Vibrant lilies in pink and white jostled with stately delphiniums. Every shade of rose and carnation nestled in bright green asparagus fern, lightened by sprays of gypsophila, like a portable rainbow.

"Here." She stopped outside a building covered with an ornate display of tiles. "If you're having breakfast in Dublin, you have to have it in Bewleys." The smell of freshly roasted coffee was so enticing Annie could almost taste it when they walked up the stairs towards the James Joyce Room. She smiled with satisfaction. Her favorite leather sofa near the open window was vacant. Perfect.

The sounds of people drifted up from the street below, a myriad of different languages in the buzz of sound. A familiar melody layered with strumming guitar part of the city's symphony. An enthusiastic street performer was trying his best, but failing miserably to reproduce one of Leonard Cohen's classics.

"I love to come here when I'm working on a new flavor. The sounds and sights inspire me. As I drink coffee I imagine what flavors I'd love to be swirling around in my mouth." It was Annie's secret. Her way of tapping into her creative side. Part of her she normally kept hidden, just for herself.

"All the different cultures meld to create the new Dublin, and yet the old Dublin is still here. I can imagine generations of people sitting here. Living in the Georgian buildings, walking in St. Stephen's Green." She grinned and took a long swallow of her coffee. "I'm getting lyrical, I need some food."

"Obviously." He passed her the basket of pastries. "You could be inspired somewhere else, you know. It doesn't have to be Dublin."

Her phone rang in the bottom of her bag. She rooted frantically through the detritus to find it, glancing at the display quickly before opening it.

"Anne Devine." This was it. She gripped the phone so tight her fingers hurt. A balloon of sunlight burst inside her chest. She put her coffee down with a shaky hand.

"That's fantastic, I can't believe it!" The caller was still speaking, more details.

"When's the presentation? Okay, 'till Friday night then. Thank you." She closed the phone.

"I'm won it Jack, I won the competition!" Elation danced through her.

THE CAFÉ WAS full of people, but Jack was only aware of Annie. His hand cupped the side of her face and she leaned in to him eagerly, her mouth opening under his instantly. He deepened the kiss and pulled her closer. A potent spell wove itself around him all over again, the urge to be alone with her growing to an almost unbearable pitch.

Reluctantly, he pulled back. Her lips were pink from his attentions; a soft flush suffused her features. Her chest underneath her soft sweater rose and fell.

"Congratulations. We should celebrate later."

She blushed, and pushed her hair away from her face with shaking fingers.

"I wish we had time to celebrate now." Her gaze flickered from his mouth to his eyes, in perfect accord. She found the idea of celebrating arousing too. He stroked her arm, then clasped her fingers in his, holding on tightly.

"I'd better get back to the flat. I can't call home from here. I'll be on for hours. Mum and Da will want to know every detail." She shoved her phone back into her bag. "I guess you have to get ready for your meeting too."

"I should have it all tied up in a couple of hours," he said. "Then we can celebrate in style."

"Okay. Sounds good." They paid and left the café. He reached for her hand again, rubbing his fingers against hers, marveling at the electricity sparking between them.

"I'll give you a lift home on the way to my meeting." It would be a chance for a few more minutes together. Although God knows how he could resist touching her again when they were back in the hotel room. He strode towards the hotel's entrance, but she held back.

"No, I've a couple of things to do before I go back to Durna." She pulled him down to her. "If I go upstairs with you now I might get distracted."

"You definitely would get distracted," he muttered against her mouth, amazed at his body's instant reaction to her nearness. "Then neither of us would get anything done."

"Later."

"Okay." He lowered his head to kiss her passionately, not caring about the crowds of people swarming past. He was too busy reveling in the softness of her mouth, and the feeling of her hand on him.

I don't want you to go.

He released her reluctantly. Fought the urge to pull her back into his arms. She took a step away and pressed four fingers to her lips, blowing him a kiss before walking away. She turned and glanced back a moment before she turned down Grafton Street. A powerful bolt of something unfamiliar struck him when their eyes connected. She smiled, and he stopped breathing.

Venus Devine, Goddess of love. She'd stolen underneath the love-proof vest covering his heart. Losing her, if only for a few hours, would be torture. He raised a hand in farewell, and helplessly watched her vanish into the crowd.

WINNING the worldwide Bateau Rouge contract would be a coup for whatever company landed it, and Jack and his team had spent months preparing their pitch. Every day Jack had kept a diary carefully evaluating the yacht's strengths and weaknesses. He'd also made a video diary, and had spent the days in Durna editing it to include in his presentation.

Now, in the Bateau Rouge boardroom he glanced around the table of directors who would decide if his small company would be the one to win the lucrative contract. The rapt faces of the board were glued to his onscreen presentation as he talked them through the first storm he'd faced. When he'd finished there was an audible buzz of excited comment from the group.

"I needed to do the voyage to get a proper feel for the yacht," he said. "I don't believe in selling something purely on the way it looks. A yacht is more than appearance. The relationship between yacht and sailor is an intimate one. I needed to capture the Bateau Rouge's essence. To feel how she handles, the way she reacts to me. The way we would work together."

There were many parallels in the way he and Annie worked. Each tried to tie down the indefinable essence that transcended the superficial.

"Only then, did I feel I knew the yacht properly. I understood why the discerning sailor would choose to invest in your product, rather than someone else's. With that knowledge, I knew how to promote it. A friend of mine once told me the Bateau Rouge is what dreams are made of."

He nodded towards an assistant who was in charge of dimming the lights in the boardroom. "Gentlemen, let me show you what we were thinking of in the way of a campaign." He delivered the presentation with practiced ease. The faces around the table altered from guarded to excited. A feeling of rightness swelled his chest. It was all going to plan. The presentation was working its magic. He'd done this often enough to know the contract was theirs, so where was the expected feeling of elation?

Moments later, he accepted thanks and shook hands with the men as they filed out. One man remained. Bateau Rouge's Managing Director.

"That was an excellent presentation, Jack." Roger MacDonald was pleased. "I think I can speak for all of us when I say we were all very impressed with your vision for our company. I'd like to thank you for taking the time to come and present it to us."

"Delighted to, Roger."

"I'll have to consult with the others, but I'll phone you in an hour and let you know." His voice lowered conspiratorially, "I can't pre-empt the decision, but…"

"I'll be waiting for your call." If it were up to the tall, dynamic man, the contract was firmly in

Miller Advertising's hands. Jack quickly stowed his laptop and strode with Roger to the building's light and airy foyer.

"Thanks again, Jack." Roger shook his hand firmly. "I'll be in touch."

Jack climbed into the car and started the engine. At two hours, the meeting had gone even quicker than expected. He needed to get back to New York and finalize the new pitch to Mecredi Cars. Frustration welled up within him at the constraints his job was placing on him. He'd only just found his long lost grandmother. Now, without the mental challenge of the presentation to distract him, his mind and body craved Annie again. There had been such joy in her face in the café. As if all of her dreams had come true.

He needed to be in New York. She seemed to think she'd got everything she ever wanted by winning this competition. He glanced into the rear view mirror, recognizing the determined look in the set of his jaw. The look Roxie told him terrified people. With his departure for New York pushed forward, there were things he needed to do.

He was just pulling up outside the nursing home when his mobile rang.

"Jack, it's Roger, we've made our decision. We'd like Miller Advertising to run the campaign."

"That's great, Roger." There was always a burst of satisfaction when he nailed a contract, but this time it was suspiciously absent.

"I'll talk to my team and we'll get things rolling." Jack ended the call, shrugging off the lingering feeling of disquiet.

He checked in at reception and asked to see Dr. Lynch.

"Mr. Miller." The doctor met him at reception and walked him into his office. "What can I do for you?"

"I want to talk about my grandmother." He sank down on the hard wooden chair. "I have to go back to New York, and I want to make arrangements to have her come live near me."

Silence.

"I'm not sure that's a good idea." The doctor leaned his elbows on the desk. Steepled his fingers. "As her doctor I certainly can't recommend it."

He needed family. Needed to belong. His grandmother needed him too. Without him, her last days would be eked out without any family to comfort her. Couldn't the doctor understand how important this was to him?

"I don't understand." There was no way he would abandon her in her hour of need. He had the financial clout to ensure his grandmother received the best care possible. "I can provide for her medical care. I'm going back to the States in a couple of days and intend to thoroughly check nursing homes over there. I'm sure I can find one which will suit her needs."

He crossed his arms. Tried not to glower.

"I'm sorry, Mr. Miller, but there's more to it than that." Dr. Lynch scratched his nose, his brow creasing as he hunted for the right words to explain himself. "The issue is not the quality of care, but familiarity. Your grandmother's Alzheimer's means she's not capable of understanding why she should leave her familiar environment. Moving her will cause her mental distress."

"I can't just leave her."

"I understand your feelings, Mr. Miller, but you must understand Mary is soothed by her familiar surroundings. The nurses understand her likes and dislikes. Know her history. Talk to her about her husband, and her daughter. She feels safe and cocooned here. Moving her would be too much. It would very definitely be to her detriment."

"But physically she would be able for the move?" Jack was unwilling to let her go. Not without a fight.

"Physically she would survive it. But mentally..." Dr Lynch didn't need to finish the sentence.

It wouldn't be fair to cause her any sort of

trauma. Especially avoidable trauma. Jack's spirits sank. He had to think of her.

"All right, Doctor. I'll have to think about what you've told me."

"She's just had her lunch. Would you like to see her? I know she enjoyed your previous visit, although I can't guarantee she'll remember you."

"I'd like to see her." On stiff legs, Jack followed the doctor to his grandmother's room.

TWELVE

Annie slumped on the sofa in her empty apartment with her business plan on her knee. She flicked it open, and scanned the paragraphs of text that she'd written detailing the next steps that her fledgling business would take. If she won. And she had.

Detailed daydreams had sketched out the next step in vivid detail. First, she'd ring her parents, and tell them. Next, she'd go down to the chocolate shop and imagine it's front transformed. A beautifully lettered sign in green and gold, stating Devine Chocolates would be covered with a matching awning. And below it, a display of her chocolates set on fine white china would entice the customers in.

She'd even had a signwriter work on some

sketches. She picked one up, and examined it, as her heart sank into her shoes. The shop had been the opportunity of a lifetime. Now the thought of it tightened like a noose. With a premises in Dublin, she wouldn't be able to explore other options. Options like going to New York with Jack, and a possibility of a future with him.

She twirled a skein of hair between her fingers, tormented.

This is what I've always dreamed of, and now I've got it, I want something else entirely. She picked up the phone and dialed home, laying the business plan down on the sofa next to her.

"Mum, it's Annie."

"Well?" She loved the way her mother got right down to the crux of the matter, not even bothering with Hello.

"I got it. I won." She held the phone away from her ear. Letting her mother's piercing scream of delight dissipate in the inches between receiver and ear.

"Oh, Darling, congratulations! I know it's everything you've ever wanted."

Annie couldn't speak. *It wasn't, it didn't even come close.*

"Are you there, Love?"

"I'm here." It was impossible to feel elated. Her stomach churned, and her heart was like a deflated balloon in her chest.

"Is Jack with you?"

"He's working, he has his presentation." *After which he's going back to his life.* Her eyes prickled with unshed tears. She hated feeling like this. So defeated and unsure.

"Can I talk to Da? I'd like to tell him about the competition."

"He's up in the pub. You know him, he decided to go in early. Why don't you call him later? I'll let you break the good news to him."

Annie hung up. A headache bloomed in her temples, bleeding into her forehead. She'd have to take a pill; this one wasn't going away on its own. Her eyes flicked open and she jumped as the door slammed.

"Hi, Annie." Her flat-mate David strolled to the fridge and glanced hopefully inside. "What's new?"

"I got it."

David closed the fridge and turned to look at her.

"The competition?"

"Yup, I won the Chocolate Oscar." She couldn't even raise a smile. The pain was spreading out to poke at the back of her eyeballs.

"What's up?" David sat down next to her. He eyed her in concern. "Somebody die?"

"No. I have a headache." Her voice sounded flat, which was hardly surprising, considering. "I always thought I'd be happy when I won. I had my whole life mapped out, the flat here with you, the shop on Grafton Street…"

"David filled a glass with water, pressed two paracetamol from the packet over the sink and brought it to her. He knew all about the shop, she'd dragged him down there often enough to look into its window, explaining all the changes she would make when she took it over.

"After I left Jack this morning I went down and looked at it. It's just perfect, but now…"

She took the pills from her cousin, swallowing them with a gulp of water. Jack had brought the misty fog of Durna with him when he'd walked over and kissed her the first time in the pub, and now everything was occluded. She didn't know what she wanted anymore.

Jack. He was coming for dinner, and there wasn't an edible thing in the house.

"What time is it?" She jumped up from the sofa and searched the cluttered table for her watch.

"Almost five." David looked guarded, she probably had her panicked look on again.

"Jack's coming for dinner."

"Oh. Is this the guy from Durna? The one with the boat?"

"How do you know about Jack?"

"Jungle drums." David grinned. "My mother

was on. Told me all about him. It's the talk of the village."

Nothing new there then.

"What are we having, or do you want me to make myself scarce?"

Annie walked across the room and hugged him.

"It's time you two met. Of course you're included." She pulled back and grinned at him. "Who do you think's doing the cooking?"

"Huh." He shrugged. "Oh well, I guess if it's going to be edible…"

"David!" She punched him gently on the arm. "There's no need to be insulting." Although to be honest, he cooked a lot better than she did. "I thought we'd go for a take-away from the deli. Will you come with me and help?"

"Okay." He grabbed his leather jacket from the back of the chair. She searched in her bag for her car keys.

"What are you looking for?"

"Keys."

"There." He pointed to the counter where she'd discarded them.

"Let's get going," he said, "Before it closes."

JACK CLIMBED INTO HIS CAR, tossing his jacket onto the backseat, and drove down to the seafront. He parked so he could look out at the grey waves breaking on the shoreline. Dialed Roxie.

The phone rang for a couple of moments before she answered.

"Roxie, it's Jack."

"Hi, how's it going?"

There were no hidden tensions in her voice, no undertones of concern. Of course Roxie had no need for concern, she'd no idea what was going on in his life, he'd never confided in her.

"I've discovered a relative I never knew I had." It was time. The secret would be out soon enough. Roxie should know. There was silence on the other end of the line. For the first time in their relationship, he'd managed to strike her dumb. "A grandmother. You'll like her." In his grandmother's room there was only one thing that was truly hers: the table of photographs. She picked them up often. Stared into the faces of the people that she'd loved who had left her. She lived with them. Lived for the past. She didn't have anyone alive who cared about her anymore. Jack had a decision to make. Was he destined to end up as a series of photographs on this table too, or would his presence in his grandmother's life be more physical than that?

Roxie was breathing, but not speaking. Not typical Roxie at all. Maybe confiding in her wasn't such a good idea.

"I need you to organize some flights for me." He gave her the details, briskly putting things back on a business footing. His phone chirped and he glanced at the screen. Dammit, he'd forgotten to charge it last night and was running out of juice.

"Just organize it for me, will you Roxie? I'm running out of battery."

He tried turning it off and on again, but the screen flickered and died.

Damn, I wanted to call Annie to let her know I'm on my way. He stuffed his useless phone into his pocket. He would be early. If she wasn't there he could wait for her in the car. He started the engine, and pulled out. Black clouds threatened, and the smell of rain hung heavy in the air. He turned up the heat, and closed the windows. When he got to her house, they could settle down and enjoy dinner. And the champagne he'd bought.

We've got a lot to celebrate. His spirits rose at the thought. *And celebrating can be fun.*

It had started to rain slowly and steadily the way it did in Ireland. He searched for a parking space, soft drops misting his windscreen. Her car was idling by the curb. Jack's heartbeat quickened. In moments, he'd be kissing her again. As he watched, Annie climbed out of the car, holding her jacket over her head and turned to the stranger who was clambering out of the passenger seat.

She was laughing, the way she laughed when she was with him. Acid burned his gut and his fingers clenched convulsively around the steering wheel. The stranger was tall, with longish dark hair, and a battered leather jacket. He grabbed a handful of bags from the back seat as Annie splashed through a puddle. He draped his arm around her and they dashed up the steps towards the door.

A yellow car pulled out in front of him. Jack pulled in to the now vacant spot, watching in his rear view mirror as the stranger slipped a key out of his pocket and deftly opened the door. He screwed his eyes up tight to banish the image of Annie's face tilted towards the stranger.

No, not a stranger. A stranger wouldn't have a key. He opened his eyes again. They'd gone inside. He pulled his fingers over his eyelids from inner corner to temple, sliding his palms over his cheeks. His mind returned to an earlier conversation. A conversation where their faces were so close together he'd felt her warm breath on his face as they'd talked.

I'm not just small village Annie, I'm also a Big City Venus. Her words echoed in his head, and even with the image of the man's arm around her shoulder burned into his retina, he couldn't force his stunned brain to accept it. A big city Venus with a separate life than the one she had in Durna.

Jack's knuckles clenched white against the black leather steering wheel. Anger and pain rose up like lava, and filled him with molten pain. He'd asked her to come to New York but she hadn't said yes. She'd told him her future was in Dublin, how stupid did he have to be, not to realize she had her eyes firmly set on a future that didn't include him? All the conversations they'd had slammed into him, like bullets.

Now my future can begin, she'd said. *A future with this guy?*

It was a new sensation, but he didn't have to be a genius to recognize it. Jealousy, wrapped in a hot glove of rage. Jack picked his jacket off the seat next to him, and slipped into it. He hadn't been alone when he'd told her he wanted to try for a relationship, he reminded himself, she'd been right there too. He'd walked away when he found Sharon had a lover, but no way would he turn around and walk away now.

The car locked with a muted beep. Jack dashed across the street. Cold rain dripped through his hair to run in little streams through his scalp.

He didn't want to catch her out, didn't want to find her snuggling under a towel with the man she lived with. He stood there anyway, waiting for the door to open.

"Jack!" She was all over him. Her hands slid over his chest and she stared into his eyes. She didn't notice his hands stayed firmly at his side.

"You're soaked!" She stood back and he stepped in stiffly, eyes casting behind her in the empty room. There was no sign of the man, but his leather jacket was slung over the chair, water dripping from it onto the floor.

"I'll get a towel." Before he had a chance to confront her she was gone, running from what he could see was a small sitting room into what he presumed must be the bathroom. Jack closed the front door quietly. There was no need to bring her neighbors into it.

She was back, rushing to him with a large blue towel clutched in her hands. Despite it all, he wanted nothing more than to forget the man he'd seen her with, the man with his arm around her. A man who'd looked like he had after three weeks at sea, a scruffy charmer. He glanced towards the spreading puddle on the floor, and her eyes followed his.

"Bloody hell." She glared at the pool of water. "David!"

A door opened next to the bathroom and the

one who must've been David appeared, pulling a dry tee- shirt over his impressive chest. "Bring an old towel out of the airing cupboard will you? Your jacket's making one hell of a mess."

"I think the mess can wait." Jack stood still, staring at her lover.

He's big, but I'm bigger. Satisfaction blazed through him. He could take him in a fight, and one was brewing. He clenched his fists at his side, ready.

"I think you need to introduce me to your friend, Annie."

IF SHE DIDN'T KNOW BETTER, Annie would swear there was steam coming off Jack as he faced David. There was a stillness in the steady way he looked at her cousin. A muscle flexed in the corner of his jaw, and his fists were clenched.

"Didn't I tell you about David?" she asked, weakly.

"No, surprisingly you omitted all mention of him. I guess we've been too busy for David's name to come up." He stared at the man with open contempt now. *He thought he was her lover.* The realization struck her like a blow to the solar plexus.

"I'm Annie's flat-mate." David said.

"David's my *cousin*," she said. "There are *two* bedrooms. His and mine." She gestured towards the doors on the other side of the small sitting room. "We've shared a flat since I left Durna."

"Cousin?" The tension released the stiffness of his shoulders instantly.

"First cousin," David grinned. "Our fathers are brothers."

"Your father is Sean?" Jack glanced at Annie.

"Yes."

Jack reached for the towel and rubbed it over his hair.

Needing time to think, Annie walked into the bathroom to retrieve an old towel to mop the moisture from the floor. Her hands shook as she pulled it out of the cupboard.

Jack hadn't tried to hide his fury. *He wasn't capable of hiding it.* He'd really thought she was living with David. Which she was, but not in the way he seemed to think.

The room was empty when she strode back in. She dropped the cloth over the spreading pool of water, then sank down onto her knees rubbing it ferociously. Jack and David were talking in the sitting room. *Bloody male bonding.* She picked up the cloth and tossed it into the sink. *He needn't think I'm going to be so easy to talk around.* She walked to the fridge and pulled out a beer, turning to rifle the drawer for the bottle opener.

"It's here." She hadn't heard him come in, still steaming at the unfairness of being unjustly accused. "We had it next door."

He approached her, crowded into her personal space, and she backed up against the fridge. Without looking he took the bottle from her hand and carefully placed it on the counter, the heat of his thighs against hers seeping through the cotton of her dress.

She moved, but he was quicker. He placed his hands flat against the fridge's surface on either side of her face, and moved so close his mouth was bare millimeters from hers.

"I'm sorry." He kissed her gently, lovingly, and despite her hurt she couldn't resist him, her mouth softening under his. "I'm sorry," he said again, against her lips before deepening the pressure. The flame burned out of control between them again and she ran her fingers around the back of his head, holding him desperately.

"I can't believe you thought David and I were living together."

"You are."

"You know what I mean," she glowered. "You thought David was my lover and I was sleeping with you. How could you think that?"

"I've told you I'm sorry, I don't know what else I can say. It was a stupid mistake."

"I thought you trusted me." Of all of the

things he might have believed her capable of, this was the one thing which hurt most. After being on the receiving end, she'd never cheat on someone.

"Why would I even pretend to be your girlfriend if I had a boyfriend of my own?"

"You told me you were a different person in Durna, had a different life."

"Yes, I guess I did, didn't I?" Pain burned in her chest. It was a lifetime ago. Before they'd slept together and everything changed completely. For her anyway. She'd thought things had moved to another level. He'd wanted her to go to New York with him for a visit. But he didn't trust her. His response to David proved it. Once again she'd made the mistake of thinking she knew what was in another persons heart. They never should have moved from a pretend relationship to a real one.

"David's in the sitting room." She suddenly remembered her cousin. "We're supposed to be all having dinner together."

"He said he's decided to take his girlfriend out for a meal. He called her, and has gone to change." She didn't trust the innocence of his gaze for a second.

"Did you..." she started.

"He made the decision all by himself. He told me he didn't fancy my chances after the way I acted earlier." He rubbed his hand across his jaw line, looking embarrassed. "He said he reckoned he'd escape the fireworks."

"Yeah, well, David and I have shared a flat for a long time," she nodded. "And I haven't forgiven you yet." She squeezed out from beneath his arm, putting distance between them and running her hands down the skirt of her dress, trying to look at least vaguely respectable.

"Annie?" David called tentatively from the sitting room.

"He sounds scared," Jack said.

"Like I said, he knows me." Annie pushed open the door from the kitchen, knowing without looking that Jack was following her.

"I've called Sophie and we're having dinner out. I'm going to stay with her tonight." His voice lowered. "Everything okay?"

"Yeah, fine." She reached up to kiss her cousin on his cheek. "I'm going back to Durna tomorrow for the ceili, are you coming up?"

"Maybe. If I can drag Sophie away, otherwise I'll stay down here." He turned to Jack, "There's nothing worse than a ceili if you're on your own."

"I'll be going with her," Jack grabbed David's proffered hand. "Hopefully see you tomorrow then."

"Right," David said then turned to Annie. "Don't forget to call home; Bull should be back from the pub."

"I'll call them now." Annie patted her cousin on the back.

He grabbed his jacket from the chair and left.

JACK SANK down on the sofa. Silence stretched between them. Annie fiddled with her hair. She was uncomfortable with him, now they were alone together. He rubbed his hands over his jean-clad thighs. His over-the-top reaction to David had ruined a potentially wonderful night.

"So, can I help you with dinner?"

"You can do more than that." She grinned. "You can do it, while I call Bull." He pulled a face, obviously she loved cooking as much as he did then.

"It's easy. We got a selection of stuff from the deli. I was going to pretend I cooked it, but you better know everything at this stage." She ran her hand through her hair, pushing it back from her face. "I'm a rotten cook. It's a well known fact my specialty is 'heat and serve'."

"My favorite. Is everything in the fridge?" He strode towards the kitchen relieved to have something to occupy him. A few moments apart to let the awkwardness dissipate couldn't be a bad thing.

"All ready to go in foil containers." She nodded, reaching for the phone.

Her voice drifted in from the sitting room as he opened the containers and heated the oven. She was laughing, reliving the telephone call she'd received earlier in the day in all its glory. He lingered in the kitchen until she was finished.

Ten minutes later, she joined him.

"Your parents must be delighted," he said.

"They are. Bull said I must be on a winning streak, what with winning the Chocolate Oscar and landing a boyfriend in the same week." There was something in her eyes, sadness maybe?

"I didn't tell him we were only pretending."

"Because we're not." They'd moved way past pretending. Even when he'd thought she was with another man he'd not been prepared to let her go. He was going to fight for Annie. If she didn't know that now, then she soon would.

"Because I don't really know what we're doing, I can't believe you thought me capable of living with someone and making love to you." Her hands clenched into fists and her determined gaze challenged him to keep his distance.

It wasn't finished then. He breathed in. He was about to dive into dangerous waters without the benefit of a spear gun or a safety cage to keep him safe.

"I can't explain it." Jack shrugged his

shoulders; he really didn't have an excuse. He'd behaved like a caveman.

"I can apologize for it, but I'm not denying when I saw him outside with his arm around your shoulders, and watched him open the door *with his key,* coherent thought took a back seat." She seemed a fraction more approachable. He took in a deep breath and opened his heart.

"I was jealous. So jealous I couldn't see straight. I've never had a woman affect me like you do." He held his breath. Nothing mattered if Annie didn't forgive him. He'd come to Ireland looking for somewhere to belong. The truth hit him like a lightning bolt. He belonged with Annie.

"It was a surprise." She took a step nearer.

"You can say that again." He pulled her close, breathing in her potent scent. His body jolted into life with her soft warmth in his arms. "You smell of vanilla." He sniffed the skin of her neck.

"It's body lotion, I put some on after my vanilla bubble bath. Vanilla's my favorite."

"Mine too." He reached for her hand and pulled her into the kitchen with him to turn off the oven. "Let's eat later." He nuzzled her neck. Her fingers reached for the bottom of his tee shirt, pulling it roughly up so she could stroke his stomach.

"I'm too hungry for you to bother with food."

"Oh, you sweet talker," she replied. She pulled

his tee shirt up and over his head. Reached for his belt buckle.

"Bedroom." Relief flooded through him, relief that she'd understood, relief she'd given him a second chance. He picked her up, striding from the kitchen with the sharp nip of her teeth at his neck inflaming him. His arms tightened behind the soft skin of her knees.

"Slow down." He stumbled as she licked his throat and barely made it to the bed. "There's a limit to what I can take."

"No good at multitasking, Jack?" She wriggled out of her dress with a half smile that turned his knees to jelly. He dropped his jeans to the ground and quickly stripped off his socks and shoes.

"I admit it," he growled. She unfastened her bra and tossed it in the direction of the lamp. "I'm only human."

"Very human."

He peeled off his white briefs to stand naked before her and her eyes widened at the proof of how very human he was.

"Come here."

"Impatient, sweetheart?" He ran his hands up her thighs to hook his fingers into the lacy scrap she doubtless called panties.

"Okay, you got me." She moaned as his lips followed the path of his hands, kissing her stomach. "I'm burning up for you."

"Good." He moved to a nipple, swirling his tongue around its hardening tip, sucking hard. She gasped, and her legs edged wider under his as his length nudged her.

"I love the way you smell." His lips trailed over her neck. His nostrils filled with the subtle scent of vanilla again and he breathed it in deeply. She arched under him, her body eloquently transmitting her desperate desire to him. "And the way your skin feels, so soft and warm." He nipped her ear lobe gently and her hands ran feverishly over his back.

"I think I'm going to explode," she whispered. "I want you now, Jack."

"Not yet. Have you any more of the body lotion?"

Her eyes widened. She pointed to the bottle on the bedside table.

"Now," he said slowly, "you've done quite a good job, but there are some parts you missed."

"There are?" She grinned. "I was pretty thorough."

"Maybe you thought you were being thorough, but believe me, you missed a bit, and you should always make sure you moisturize properly after a bath." He poured the lotion into his palm. The subtle fragrance of vanilla permeated the air.

"Did you rub it on your stomach?" The

muscles on his face twitched with the effort of keeping his face straight.

"I may have forgotten." His hands smoothed over the soft skin. She moaned and squirmed under his hands.

"Thought so." He knelt next to her and his fingers worked their magic.

"Just relax," he whispered. Her fists clutched at the bedspread. His hands swept over her thighs, then up to caress her breasts, carefully working the lotion into them.

"Jack," she moaned. He carefully turned her over, pouring more lotion into his hands.

"You can't have done here." His hands were gliding over her back, slipping lower to caress her bottom.

"My legs..." His fingers stilled for an enchanted moment, then slid down the back of her thighs, massaging them firmly.

"Just your feet now." He reached for the bottle again, but she captured his wrist with an impatient hand, turning in the circle of his arms.

"My feet can wait." She reached up and pulled his head down to hers.

"But I can't." She nipped his bottom lip, and the ravenous need she was feeling blazed through him as their mouths met hungrily.

THIRTEEN

Jack's arm tightened around Annie in sleep. *If there's anything better than this, I don't know what it is.* She glanced at the clock on the bedside table. It was late, and they hadn't eaten. Her stomach grumbled loudly in protest. *God, I'm starving!*

"Are we being attacked by the Hound of the Baskervilles, or are you hungry?" Jack's big body flexed. She wanted him again. How on earth was that possible?

"Hungry." She wriggled out from under his arm and pulled on her bathrobe. "I'm going to heat up dinner, I missed lunch."

He linked his fingers behind his head and smiled at her.

"You look good in there." If truth be told, he

looked *right* there in her bed. Her stomach growled loudly again and she covered it with her outspread fingers in embarrassment.

"But food calls, right?" he teased. "Go heat it up and I'll have a quick shower."

She nodded, and escaped into the kitchen. If she waited to see him climb out of bed there was no way she would be able to resist climbing right back into bed with him.

She pulled the salad things from the fridge and mixed balsamic vinegar and olive oil into a vinaigrette. Her mouth watered as she chopped avocado and tomatoes, and ripped lettuce, arranging it all in a colorful bowl and adding a handful of flaked almonds before drizzling the vinaigrette over.

Time was running out. Only one more week and then the festival would end with the festival party. With a start she remembered Jack's meeting. Her fingers stilled. She hadn't even asked him about the presentation. She'd been so distracted by the vision of his eyes blazing as he challenged David, and then… Annie caught a glance of herself in the mirrored front of the microwave, and peered closer. Her hair was standing on end and she had the stupidest smile plastered over her face. She ran fingers through her hair, trying to smooth it.

"There's no point, it's beyond repair." Jack was fully dressed again. The wet hair combed back from his face accentuating killer cheekbones.

"I didn't ask you about the meeting." She pulled the food out of the oven and set it up on the pine table, while he pulled out two plates and cutlery.

"I got it." He said quietly. "We're going to be handling the account. I went to see Mary afterwards. I wanted to talk to her doctor about moving her to New York."

"I'm really happy for you, Jack; it looks like your trip across the Atlantic was worth it then."

"It was definitely worth it, Annie. Without the lightning strike, I never would have stopped at Durna."

"And ended up at a matchmaking festival." She laughed shakily. He was planning to take Mary away with him. There'd be no need for him to stay. Emotion burned through her chest at the thought of Jack leaving, back to his life and work in New York. "It'll make one hell of a dinner party story."

His eyes flashed and he crowded into the space between them. "You and me are no dinner party story." He wrapped his arms around her and kissed her hard. So hard she was breathless.

"I didn't mean…"

"What did you mean?" his eyebrows lowered and anger flared in his eyes, transmuting them to navy. "It sounded like you were saying what we had was only a temporary thing." His eyes narrowed. "Have you had enough of me?"

There was something about the set of his shoulders and the way he held himself. As if steeling himself for a blow. He was closed off and defensive, protecting himself.

From me? From something I'd say?

She laid her palm flat on his chest, feeling the constricted muscles twitch under her palm.

"I don't think I'll ever have enough of you," she admitted huskily.

His eyes locked with hers, questioning then believing the truth of her words. The tension in his features released, and the Jack she knew re-emerged. The Jack, who in so few days had become so achingly familiar. So vital, somehow, to her survival.

Her arms slid around his neck, pulling him down for her kiss. The light caress was so tender she felt the prick of tears behind her closed lids.

She sighed, as his fingers cupped her nape.

"Do you have your passport?"

The sudden change of subject jolted her. Her eyes shot open and she stared up at him, uncomprehending.

"Passport?"

"I've booked us on a flight tomorrow lunchtime." He walked across the room and flicked on the kettle, all business now. "You can pack in the morning and then we can pick up my bags from the hotel."

"To New York," she whispered weakly.

"I've a few things to organize." He measured coffee grounds into the cafetiere, and followed it with boiling water. "I have to get this problem with Mecredi Cars sorted out."

"Mecredi Cars?" She shook her head, trying to spark her speech centre into consciousness, all it seemed to be capable of was parroting whatever he said.

"My client." He took milk out of the fridge. "I have to make a new presentation."

Her mouth gaped. Jack had covered miles while she progressed by inches, and the unbelievable leaps he'd made without even consulting her rendered her speechless.

He poured coffee into two mugs and held one out for her. She took it from him soundlessly. It was all moving too fast. Out of control. He wanted her to come with him, but she couldn't leave now. It was impossible.

"I can't go," she declared. "There's no way. The ceili is tomorrow and it's such a lot of work we have to get everyone involved to help. I promised Da I'd be there for it."

"It's just a dance, isn't it? I'm sure someone else can help." He brushed it off like lint from a jacket.

"The presentation for the Chocolate Oscars is on Friday." The culmination of all her hard work. The pinnacle of professional achievement.

"Do you have to go?"

"Yes, I have to go!" *How could he not know what winning meant to her?*

"It's my life, Jack. It's everything I've worked toward. Everything I've dreamed about!" *And Jack wants me to forget all about it; it doesn't matter to him at all.*

He'd spoken about moving his grandmother. Had he even asked Mary what she wanted, or had he made a unilateral decision there too?

"You talked to your grandmother's doctor. About moving her to America."

He nodded, and drank his coffee calmly. "I want her to be with me."

"What did the doctor say, Jack? What does he think about you relocating her?"

"He said it wasn't in her best interest." His jaw clenched. The doctor's advice must have been unwelcome. He looked furious. It was as if he was so used to getting his own way he wasn't capable of taking someone else's feelings into account. Someone else's needs.

"But you're planning to move her anyway." There wasn't any point in shouting, he wasn't going to listen to her. He glared at her stubbornly and didn't reply. "I know you want family, Jack, but you have to think of what's best for her. Have you even taken her life into account while you're rejigging yours to make room for her?"

Little prickles of heat flooded her face. Despite his warning look she was too far gone to back down now. She'd known Jack was arrogant, but this went beyond arrogance, this was right up there in control freak territory.

"And your life too, I suppose." He slammed his mug down on the table. "I'm only asking you to come for a visit."

"You're not asking, you're telling. You're organizing my life without even finding out what I think about it." She turned away from him, pain welling up in her chest. She'd spent the afternoon struggling with tortuous thoughts of what she might have to give up in order to have a relationship with Jack. Whatever she was going to do would be *her* decision.

"I won't be told what to do, Jack, I'm never giving over control of my life again."

"Is this about your wedding?" he asked,

"Being left at the altar? Because I didn't leave you at the altar, Annie. It was a long time ago."

"So get over it? Is that what you're saying?"

She glanced around for something to throw. He had it coming.

"Yes. You're not the only one who lost out, he lost out too."

"Because he ended up with my friend, not me." She frowned at him cynically; she had no idea where he was going with this one.

"Because he left his home, and she did too, and I'm guessing they haven't shown their faces in Durna since."

She stopped dead. He was right, neither of them had returned.

"So, that's two families torn apart. Just so you're not upset." He strode towards the door. "It's not just your parents who look after you, it's the whole town." He stared into her eyes with fury in his. "And they do it because you let them. You play the victim card. I'm going to the hotel to pack, I have a flight tomorrow morning." The door slammed loudly behind him, and she stumbled towards the window just in time to see him accelerating away. The deep roar of the engine faded into nothingness. He drove away, out of her life.

"A WHISKEY," he ordered, sliding onto the polished chrome barstool. "And some nuts, if you have them."

The waiter nodded, placing a glass before him and a small jug of water. He turned to make elaborate cocktails for the two girls who waited next to him. Jack had thought about ordering room- service, but given up on it, too wound up by their argument to sit in the cold sterility of the suite.

"Hi, are you waiting for someone?" A tall blonde, a perfect soldier for the blonde army, eyed him with a look he knew only too well. In the past, he might have been tempted. Now, with Annie in his bloodstream, he was in no mood for female company.

"Yes, she'll be here in a moment." He picked up his glass and retreated to a shadowy booth in the corner like a bear retreating into its cave. Annie's words replaying in an endless loop in his tired brain.

You're planning to move her anyway. He threw back the whiskey. She hadn't even listened to his side of things, but had jumped to conclusions without waiting to hear what he had to say. He'd made the decision Mary couldn't be moved, and the repercussions hurt like hell. To know his grandmother, he'd have to reorganize his entire life.

He caught the eye of a waitress, and ordered a double. The cold burn of anger faded to melancholia. The last thing he should have done was walk out. Annie had such issues with abandonment, and it hadn't just been Steve, had it? The bridesmaid had betrayed her too. His head pounded and he threw back the fiery liquid with a growl. He should have stayed and forced her to listen to his side of things.

The bar was full of laughing groups of people, men and women flirting and leaning closer. Being here was even worse than being alone. With a snort of disgust, he drained his drink and tossed some notes on the table. He strode upstairs to the room. At least there, he could be miserable in peace.

ANNIE PADDED INTO THE KITCHEN. She reached up into the top cupboard, and pulled down the bottle of Cinzano. She grabbed ice from the freezer and clinked two cubes into a tall glass. She snagged a half-full bottle of lemonade from the fridge door, and she was in business.

She walked back into the sitting room, flipping open the phone. No messages, and no missed calls either. She scrolled through her contacts, staring at his number. Her finger hovered over the call button for a moment before she tossed it onto the sofa in disgust. Ice clinked against her teeth as she drank. Her mind ran over their angry exchange like a CD on repeat. None of it mattered. He was gone.

She strode into the bedroom and packed a small suitcase, needing to get away from the scene of the crime.

The pillow was still dimpled with the indent of his head. In her imagination, she could see him still lying there, arms behind his head, staring at her.

I love him.

It shouldn't have been a surprise, but somehow it was. She climbed under the covers. The pillow smelled of him, and she hugged it to her chest. Breathing him in with every breath. She longed for the feel of his body against hers with a bittersweet sadness. The man she loved had walked away. And what was worse, she'd let him. She tossed the pillow across the room. He'd accused her of playing the victim, and maybe he was right. But no more. Resolve hardened as she made plans for the day ahead. With or without Jack, she had some changes to make in her life. Starting tomorrow.

BY THE TIME Annie arrived in Durna the following morning the sun was up. When she'd started out, black clouds had hung threateningly in the air, but now a stiff wind was blowing them away. The golden glow of the sun warmed her face through the windscreen. She pushed open the door and went in, relief flooding her at seeing her mother sitting at the table with a large mug of tea.

"Hi, Mum."

"You're early!" Maeve got to her feet, immediately enveloping her in a hug. "We weren't expecting you till this afternoon!"

She glanced behind Annie. Looking for Jack.

"Jack has to go back to America. Some work emergency." She sat down on her favorite chair.

"How's things?" Maeve asked quietly. She pushed a cup of tea toward Annie and waited. Silence stretched between them. Was Jack right? Did everyone think she was still pining over Steve and Eileen's betrayal, even two years later?

"We had a fight, I don't know if we can fix it."

Maeve drank, waiting for her to continue.

"Tell me about Steve and Eileen, Mum."

"Well, you know they got married, and she's had a baby." Maeve eyed her curiously. "They're living in Galway. I didn't tell you because I didn't want to open up old wounds…"

"It's a long time ago, I'm over it." When Steve had walked away she'd thought she'd felt pain. It was a hangnail compared to the amputation of Jack's desertion.

"Having to tell everyone at the church it was over was so traumatic for you. It wasn't fair. Everybody blamed them. They still do." Maeve's mouth twisted. She'd always guarded her only child like a lioness protecting her young.

"I guess everyone's thought of me as a victim." The truth reflected in her mother's eyes stung. "I should have stayed, instead of running off to Dublin."

"Everyone has their problems, Darling," Maeve reached out to pat her hand. "But it makes it easier if you talk about them, otherwise…"

"Otherwise people don't know you've worked through it. And you've moved on." She finished Maeve's sentence.

"Yes," Maeve nodded. "We haven't discussed it, or Steve, since the wedding." She gathered her daughter into a hug.

"Things have moved on now. You have Jack."

Tears threatened. *Not any longer.* She should have called him. Tried to make him see it wasn't fair to relocate his grandmother. Tried to work it out. Instead, he'd got on the plane alone.

Things had changed since the festival, since Jack had announced he was her boyfriend. People were friendlier, more open. They were able to talk to her about their own problems in love because there was no possibility of brushing up against a sensitive subject and opening old wounds.

Jack was right, damn him.

I've been so caught up with what people think about me, I haven't taken the time to see what's going on in their lives. After the festival was over things were going to be different. She was going to act differently.

The kitchen door opened.

"Ah, Annie, you're here!" her father made his way to the table. "So, you got it." Bull nodded his approval. "We knew you would, your mother and me. We knew there wasn't anyone on the island who could make chocolates better than you."

"Anyone anywhere." Maeve doctored a cup of tea with just the right amount of milk and handed it over to her husband.

"There's a presentation on Friday, I hope you can come down for it, I'll drive you down."

"There's a lot more than a carful of us going, when I told them in the pub yesterday Niall started talking about getting a bus load together."

"Really?" She couldn't believe it. A large smile spread across her face.

"For sure," Maeve said, "They were cheering in the pub, and it turned into a real hooley. It was just a shame you weren't here. Everyone's delighted for you, Love."

Annie rubbed her eyes, surreptitiously wiping away the trace of tears.

"That's lovely." She stared into her cup, willing the tears away. "So tell us, how did the matchmaking go? Can I have a look at the book?"

"Of course you can, there 'tis." He pushed it close.

She pulled the book to her and flicked through the pages, stopping at Jack's handwriting. The bold strokes of the letters flowed over the page, so different from the small, tight writing preceding it. A picture of Noel was pasted in at the top left corner. She started to read the entries, beginning with her own.

Noel is 29 and works in farming. He'd like to meet someone who is interested in cinema and walking. He's quiet.

Then Jacks more flamboyant hand took over, *Noel loves Yeats, and has a great sense of humor. He's not ambitious, just happy to make enough to see him comfortably through life. The thing he'd like to do more than anything is go around the world, so he can immerse himself in new cultures, and see new things. He's been in love before, and knows that when love goes wrong, it hurts. But he's ready to take a chance on love again. He wants to meet a new lady who he could walk over the hills with while they explore the interests they have in common, and the ones they don't.*

She smiled. He'd described Noel exactly. It had taken Jack's probing to reveal the truth about the quiet man she'd known all her life. The details of his date with Annabel were written in, together with a postscript written in Bull's distinctive print.

Matched.

She looked up at Bull. "Is he really?"

"He is for now," said Bull. "These days, *for now* is all I can predict."

"Relationships are difficult." Maeve nodded. "You can't just take a relationship for granted. You have to work at it."

"Unless you're married to me," Bull added. Maeve raised her eyebrows, staring him down until he started to quake with laughter.

Noel gazed from the photograph with open honesty. *He's been in love before, and knows that when love goes wrong, it hurts.* She re-read Jack's words. Her father, with years of experience could only say a couple were matched 'for now'. If he couldn't tell, there was no one in the world who could say if love would last forever. She ran a finger over Jack's handwriting, loving its sweeps and dips.

He'd booked a ticket without consulting her, and told her some home truths she needed hearing years ago, if truth be told.

You can't just take a relationship for granted; you have to work at it. Her mother's words resounded in her head. Jack was an alpha male who needed to stop controlling everything and everyone. He was also a man who wanted to take their relationship to another level. He'd booked her a ticket to New York so she could experience his life, like he'd experienced hers. She already knew she loved him. Was she truly ready to throw away their relationship without trying?"

FOURTEEN

Annie hefted the cardboard box full of bunting to decorate the dance floor out of the trunk and onto her hip and staggered toward the village hall. Noel saw her coming and hurried to help.

"We'll put these up." He took the box out of her arms and carried it to where Annabel waited next to a ladder in the corner. The hall swarmed with busy people, and her ears filled with the buzz of sound, amplified by the hard wooden floor. Jack was right. She wasn't needed after all. Every job that needed doing was being done. Enthusiastically. Annie bit down on her lip and pushed open the door to the quiet outside. As she walked over the grass, the buzz of voices faded into the distance. She prodded a dry patch of grass with her foot, and then sank down on it, gripping her knees tightly to her.

The sea was calm. Light flickered off the water, and seagulls shrieked and dove overhead. She plucked a long strand of grass from the ground next to her, stripping off the sheath, picking at it with her fingers. The exposed inside was milky green. She brought it to her lips and sucked it, the soft sweet taste bringing her right back to childhood.

A little white yacht bobbed on the waves. As she breathed in the fresh sea air a feeling of rightness settled in her heart. It wasn't too late; it wouldn't be too late until the little boat set sail, without her.

She jumped as her mobile rang, and pulled it out of her pocket. It was Jack. He must be calling from the airport.

"Hello, Jack." Her heart turned over.

"Hi, Annie." The wind was picking up. Surfers were running into the water to catch the foam topped waves.

"I need to talk to you. The way we left things…"

"It wasn't right." Without his face in front of her, it was easier to lay her feelings bare. He'd already left, she had nothing to lose.

"No. It wasn't. I acted like a child. I should have stayed and talked it out. There's a lot you didn't understand. A lot I didn't tell you." A blond surfer climbed up on his board, riding the wave towards the shore. "I'm sorry I left. I won't do it again."

Warmth bloomed in her chest. There were problems between them, but if he was willing to talk them through, she was too. It was just unfortunate that they'd have to wait until he got back from New York.

"Will you call me when you're coming back?"

"I'm coming back now. I'll be with you in five minutes." The line went dead. He must think she was still in the flat. She'd gotten up before daybreak to head home. Driving through the dark beat lying in her lonely bed fretting over things hands down.

She flipped the phone open to call him back, then her fingers stilled on its buttons at the familiar purr of a large engine. Her heart leapt into her mouth as she turned from the sea.

Jack climbed out of the BMW and strode towards her. His eyes blazed with fire as he halted before her.

"How did you know I was here?" Her heart was beating so fast her head swam with the power of it. Jack. No longer a disembodied voice, but here, in the flesh.

"You told me about the ceili."

She nodded. She'd forgotten.

"I thought you had a flight to catch."

"I changed it." He stepped closer. "I've rescheduled it for tonight. From Galway." Her head tilted up to meet his gaze. "For one."

"Let's walk." She grasped his hand and tripped down the little path meandering over the cliff top, joy that he was with her lightening her steps. Soft, springy purple heather brushed at their ankles. At a secluded spot, sheltered from the wind, they settled down on a spot of grass. Her heart expanded with happiness when Jack draped an arm over her shoulders.

"I told you I wanted my grandmother to come and live with me."

Annie held her breath. This was where their conversation had taken such a desperate turn the night before. She was determined not to interrupt this time.

"And I told you what her doctor suggested, and how disappointed I was. What I didn't tell you was that I accepted his decision. It wouldn't be fair to make Mary move. This is the only home she's ever known. I told the doctor I'd have to think of something else."

And she'd accused him of not caring about his grandmother. Of thinking only of himself. No wonder he'd been so angry. She'd misjudged him.

"I got it wrong," she whispered. "I'm sorry."

"No. You were right. I did want Mary to

move. And I was damned angry when the doctor told me I couldn't have my way. It took the long drive to your house to convince me I had to put her needs before mine."

He stroked the side of her face, running his thumb over her bottom lip. Passion flared and set her body alight.

"I'm considering relocating to Ireland."

"But what about your work? The company needs you, that's why you're going back after all, isn't it?"

Hope danced in her chest, lit her eyes with its magical glow. Perhaps they did have a future together.

"Our clientele has just become international. Now I've clinched the Bateau Rouge deal. I want to reorganize things, take a business partner. I've been thinking about spending more time here."

Her hair blew across her face and he smoothed it back. The warmth of his hand caressed the back of her neck as he propelled her face towards his. Their kiss was everything she'd known it would be.

"I want to be here with you. To give our relationship a chance." They hadn't mentioned love yet, but it was just a matter of time. He'd loved his parents and they'd died. If they spent more time together she felt sure he'd realize the emotion which drew them together had a name, and its name was love.

"I do too." She kissed him right back.

"HAVE you time for a dance before you have to get your plane?" She led him by the hand back to the hall. A circle of daisies crowned her hair; the little flowers a perfect complement to her natural beauty. Her dimple winked. The prospect of a dance was enticing. It would be a chance to hold her close, move his body against hers. They had so little time he hadn't managed to sneak her away for a quiet session in the dunes.

"You know I do. A slow dance anyway." He nuzzled her neck. Kissed the vanilla scented skin. If he were creating a chocolate in homage to her, he'd use dark chocolate streaked with gold leaf to mimic the colors woven through her thick swathe of hair. It would be flavored with the finest Madagascan vanilla, to match the rest of her. He made a mental note to tell her sometime. She could call it the 'Venus.'

"Most dances in the ceili are slow ones during the festival." She wriggled, laughed at the feel of his chin on her delicate skin. "The dance of love."

"Ah. The dance of love." The smile faded

from his face, replaced by raw desperation to have her body tight against his in the twilight darkness.

"Let's go dance."

There were people everywhere. Despite Annie's declaration, the music was fast and loud, couples hurling each other across the dance floor like missiles. It seemed to be breaking the ice anyway. Laughter filled the air.

"Oh my God. This can't be the dance of love, can it?"

"More like the dance of broken bones." She grinned and jerked him out of the danger zone.

"There'll be a slow one next. Come on, let's get a drink."

At the punchbowl, a familiar giant was chatting to a small, pretty woman he hadn't met before.

"Jack, this is my cousin Michael and his wife Grainne."

Jack nodded. "Michael and I have met. But this is the first time I've met Grainne." He stuck out his hand and shook hers. "Pleased to meet you, Grainne."

"Likewise." She had an open and friendly face. "Michael's told me all about you."

Annie was looking puzzled. Her gaze flicked between them. Of course, she didn't know about Michael coming to the house on ladies night. The night he'd brought the supplies for the boat. The night he and Bull had discovered Michael's secret.

His heart fell. He hadn't told her Michael's secret. But he'd told Bull hers. He closed his eyes in dread. Waiting for the blade to fall.

The music changed, softened into a ballad. The mournful lilt of the singer perfectly matching his mood.

"Annie, they're playing our song."

Her eyes opened wide.

"Okay, it might not be 'our song' but it's the first slow one. So you're dancing with me." He did the whole macho thing of leading her out into the middle of the dance floor. He had to get her away before Michael let something slip. Jack pulled Annie into his arms and breathed in the fragrance of her hair. Her body molded itself to his in a sweet torment. He couldn't give in to it. He had to talk to her before anyone else did.

"Annie." She moved sensuously against him, swaying in the circle of his arms. It was torture. "Annie." Sharper. Her steps faltered and she cracked open her eyes to gaze up at him. "I need to talk to you about something."

SHE STILLED IN HIS ARMS. This was it. He was going to say he loved her. She just knew it.

She breathed in. It was the perfect ending of a perfect day. Her thoughts tumbled over each other, working out the details, mile a minute. He'd go back to New York for a few days and be back before the festival was over. And all the time she'd be thinking of him. Planning out the future they'd live together. Maybe they could buy somewhere in Dublin, somewhere near his grandmother, close enough so they could sail back here for holidays.

She waited.

"While you were in Dublin I spoke to your father." He didn't look happy. In fact he looked so serious she almost interrupted before remembering what had happened the last time she'd jumped in. He'd spoken to Bull? Had he asked her father for his blessing? It was archaic, but she felt sure Bull would have approved.

She nodded, silently willing him to continue.

"Did Bull tell you?" His brow creased in a fascinating puzzle of wrinkles.

"No. He didn't. Why don't you?" She smiled. He obviously needed some encouragement.

"Oh." His face fell. He was really milking the moment for all it was worth. She was happy enough to let him. It wasn't every day she got proposed to on the dance floor.

"I spoke to your father about you being the next matchmaker." The swirling couples and the mournful music faded away. She felt her jaw drop open, like a cartoon character. *It couldn't be true.*

"What?" Her legs were barely holding her up. She needed to sit down, quick. She stumbled and his hands gripped her upper arms steadying her.

"Let's sit down and talk."

She glanced around the room full of romancing couples. They sat on chairs around the dance floor, talking and flirting.

"Outside." Her feet couldn't rush her out of there quickly enough, but she resisted the urge to run. Outside, she sank down onto one of the chairs set up under the darkening sky.

Annie's hands twisted and squeezed in her lap. She bit the inside of her mouth, one part of her not wanting to hear the details, the other desperate to. Jack's voice was low as he started talking.

"I met Michael during ladies night. Later, Bull, Michael and I were talking. Michael wanted to help out matchmaking during the festival. His lifelong dream is to be a matchmaker. Bull told him he could help, but that the job of matchmaker had to come to you. It was your legacy as his only child. Michael was disappointed. Even though he'd always known you would inherit the mantle. He told Bull he'd be happy to help. I couldn't let Bull turn him down. Not when I knew you didn't want the job. I insinuated that you didn't want it. You know you dread it." He reached for her hand again, but Annie shifted in the seat, rejecting his touch. She stared out at the water. It was unforgivable. He'd betrayed her trust. Spoken to her father against her wishes.

"Isn't it time for you to be going?" There was cold anger in her stare. "You don't want to miss your plane."

"Annie, don't be like this..." There was a warning note in his voice, but she ignored it. Not this time. This was a step too far.

"You betrayed me, Jack. I asked you not to say anything. Did you even think of that when you decided to take matters into your own hands and tell him my innermost thoughts?"

He was silent.

"Well, did you?" His betrayal hurt. No, more than that, her entire body ached as if mugged. Especially her heart.

He glanced at his watch and cursed aloud.

"I have to go otherwise I'll miss my flight. If I miss this one, I'll miss my meeting. I can't stay, Annie. If we lose the contract it could be catastrophic for the company."

"Just go, Jack." *Walk away. And don't bother coming back.* She told herself she'd survive, and she knew she would. But she wouldn't be happy. She didn't think she would ever be happy again.

"I'm going. But I'll be back. Think about it while I'm gone. I'll be back for the end of festival party." He bent down and brushed her unresponsive lips with his warm ones. "This isn't over. I care about you, Annie. I'm not giving up."

His long legs rushed him to the car in moments. She sat in the dark and watched the lights of his car grow smaller until they finally faded into the distance.

FIFTEEN

The fact his office had the perfect view over Central Park didn't interest Jack in the slightest. He buzzed Roxie and asked her to come in. "Did you book the restaurant?"

Roxie and Mark were having dinner with him tonight. They were leaving straight from work. The pile of paperwork on his desk was steadily shrinking. It now resembled a small hill, rather than the mountain it had been when he returned to the office three days ago.

"Yes, it's all arranged." She'd brought her notebook in with her. She always did. Usually when he called he'd need her to. Not this time though.

"Sit for a couple of minutes, will you?"

She tossed back her shining cap of black hair.

Sat on the white leather chair opposite his and crossed her long, elegant legs. She was uncharacteristically quiet. "Will you need me to take notes this evening?"

He'd never taken his secretary for dinner before. Apart from meetings when they would be discussing a client's requirements. She'd always had to combine the tasks of eating with note taking. He was a terrible boss.

"This evening is just for us all to talk. We won't need your notebook." Jack ran a finger around his collar, loosening the fit. He hated the constriction around his neck. Being in Durna, he'd quickly got used to jeans and tee-shirts. And talking about his feelings.

"The meeting went well?" Roxie's eyebrows raised questioningly, giving her a slightly startled look. She tilted her head sideways like a curious rabbit. She must be wondering where her driven boss had gone. The aimless man facing her bore very little resemblance.

He nodded. "Yes." He'd worked with Mark to redo the presentation, and had let Mark give it. Jason Mecredi wanted him there, but Jack had insisted on only sitting in as an observer. Mark was running the show. It wasn't fair of the client to dismiss Mark's efforts. Jack had made that quite clear to Jason in a phone call before the presentation. Mark was a damn good worker. He had vision and style. There was no way Jack would take that away from him. After an hour of presentation and the subsequent discussion, Mecredi Cars announced they were satisfied. Miller Advertising had won another prestigious contract. He should be bouncing off the walls. Instead, his thoughts returned unerringly to Durna, and to Annie.

"I want you to know there are going to be some changes."

Roxie crossed and uncrossed her legs. She was nervous. Everyone dreaded change.

"In a good way," he hastily added. "I want to talk to you and Mark because I consider you both the most important people in the company. I'd like you to think about taking on a bigger role, Roxie." She'd always talked about becoming a creative, and Mark was all for it. Roxie's knowledge of the company's workings had been invaluable while he was away. She'd more than proved herself able for the job.

"Mark agrees. He was very impressed with your work while I was away. The company is expanding. I've offered Mark a directorship and he's agreed. We'd like you to take the position of Mark's assistant. Eventually take on clients on your own. When you feel ready, of course." She was beaming at him. Not smiling, actually beaming. "We'll have to employ someone to take over your position, and you'll need to spend some time training them in. Then you'll be working with Mark. It's one of the things we'll be discussing this evening. I just wanted to give you a heads up."

The other item on the agenda was his determination to take the organization global. Starting with Ireland. He would break the news over dinner.

Roxie pushed her hair behind her ears. It was only just long enough. She pulled in a deep breath. "I'd love that, Jack. You know it's what I've always wanted."

He nodded; she'd never been shy about stating her goals. "You deserve it, Roxie. You've worked hard and you're a real credit to the company."

He walked around the desk and offered her his hand. "Now, let's see if Mark is ready to go. I think we can close up early today. Don't you?"

AFTER A HELLISH COUPLE OF DAYS, Susan Goff rang to make Annie an offer she couldn't refuse. The chance to have samples of her winning chocolates grace every table at the presentation ceremony. The organizers had produced small, two-chocolate sized boxes with

Devine Chocolates printed on top. Along with acres of violet ribbon to dress them.

It was an impossible task to complete in her kitchen at home, and they'd cleverly provided the perfect solution. A miniature army of six professional chocolatiers from the catering college had been provided, along with everything they'd need. The hellish part was that there were one hundred and fifty guests. The resulting nightmare of producing a mountain of chocolates had been one unforgettable experience.

Now, one hundred and fifty boxes filled with her winning entry sat on a side table ready to be placed out onto the tables at the end of the meal. The guests were a hand picked, select group of international buyers and restaurateurs. All of whom would be tasting her chocolates before the night was through. As well as the publicity and substantial check, getting her chocolates in front of the buyers would be the catalyst to getting her company off the ground. She should be feeling ecstatic. Instead, she was exhausted.

She was stacking the final boxes on the side table when a tall, elegant lady dressed in a flowing silk dress walked up to her. "Annie? I'm Susan Goff." Annie placed the boxes down carefully. "Miss Goff." Speech deserted her in the face of the illustrious judge.

"Susan." She cast an expert eye over the

boxes, then gestured to a chair. "Call me Susan. They look fantastic." They sank onto two chairs abutting the nearest table. "I wanted to get a chance before the ceremony to meet you. To find out if you have any concerns that need my attention." Susan Goff's long red nails lay in her lap. Her tone was so warm, Annie relaxed instantly.

"I did want to talk to you about something." She pulled in a deep breath. "The shop."

One of Susan's eyebrows rose. It was an impressive trick.

"I wanted to know what would happen if I decided not to take it."

The eyebrow fell, and Susan leant closer. "In the event of you not taking the shop, we would have to award it to the runner-up. You would still be the winner of the competition, of course, but the lease for the current tenant runs out in a month, and such prime property..." She hissed out a breath. "Well, we couldn't leave it empty. Are you planning not to take us up on our offer?"

It was late in the day for making such a momentous decision, but she needed to explore all her options.

"I haven't decided yet." Her eyes clouded and she clenched her jawline tight. "I'll let you know by the end of next week."

A SUMPTUOUS SUITE of rooms formed part of Annie's prize. It was decked out with fruit, flowers and champagne. The two-roomed suite meant her parents could stay the night in luxury too, which had been a relief. Her flat was too small to accommodate them, and she didn't want them traveling back to Durna so late. It was a long drive. Annie soaked in a leisurely bath and got dressed.

The extension rang just as she was putting the final touches to her hair. She'd decided to put it up in honor of the occasion, and was fiddling with the jeweled hair chopsticks she'd bought on holiday. The mauve butterflies made of Swarovski crystal were a perfect match to her dress.

"Hello?"

"We're in the lobby. Can we come up?" It was a relief to hear Maeve's voice. Annie'd been so alone over the past couple of days. Up to her elbows in chocolate. So busy she'd not had time to brood over Jack.

"Come on up." She gave up on the hair chopsticks and opened the door, gazing down the corridor to the lift. Mum could do her hair when she arrived. Tonight, Annie was all thumbs.

The last thing she expected when she walked down into the lobby was the small throng of supporters from Durna. They'd staked out the bar and broke into spontaneous applause when they saw her.

"Surprise," Maeve said quietly. She patted her daughter's arm. "We all came down together. Dad and I are staying the night, but the rest are flying back after the presentation."

"Flying?" How could they afford that?

"Jack chartered a plane from Galway. He rang and told us to bring everyone." Maeve's face lit up. "It was wonderful, Annie. He organized a coach to bring us all here from the airport."

Annie couldn't believe it. So many people. Here. For her. Jack had known how important it was to share all this with her friends. Even when she hadn't. She sank into the throng and accepted congratulations from everyone. This evening would be everything she'd dreamed of and more. There was only one person missing. Jack. She straightened her spine and gratefully accepted a glass of champagne. This evening was about fulfilling old dreams. When Jack came back at the end of festival for the party, she'd fulfill her new ones.

THE LAST NIGHT of the festival was always the best, and this year was no exception. Early evening sunlight was still bouncing off the rocks outside the pub, and Niall had strung lanterns from the trees to bring the festival ambience outside. Inside the pub, a makeshift stage had been rigged up. A local band played enthusiastically to the growing crowd, many of whom were dancing on the space cleared in the center for exactly that purpose. A great cheer went up as Annie and Bull walked to the open doorway. When they reached the matchmaker's table a couple of drinks arrived in front of them instantly.

"On the house." Niall grinned. "With my compliments. You've brought enough business my way over the past couple of weeks."

"Thanks, Niall." Annie's eyes searched the crowd for Jack. There was no sign of him, but she knew he'd be there, he'd promised. Jack wasn't one for reneging on a deal.

Bull was deep in conversation with a group of his old friends, completely in his element. She felt a familiar tingle of watching eyes, and glanced at the doorway. Her cousin Michael stood there, unsure.

"Michael!"

He tentatively crossed the room toward her. "Hi Annie." He eyed her carefully.

"We need to talk, Michael." He pulled up a chair. "Da says you're interested in matchmaking and you've helped him while I was down in Dublin."

"I don't want you to think I was muscling in." Michael's eyes skittered away. He looked like he wanted to avoid this conversation more than *anything*.

She pulled in a breath, *here goes*. "To be honest, it would mean the world to me if you were."

He stared at her, as if unable to believe what he was hearing.

"I've always known there has to be a Devine matchmaker for the festival, and as I haven't any brothers or sisters I've always felt it should be me." Michael started to interrupt but she held up her hand to stop him. "Hear me out, Michael, please. Our grandfather was the matchmaker. Matchmaking is in your blood as well as mine, and you have both a liking and an aptitude for it. I'd consider it an honor if you were to become the next matchmaker instead of me. You're a Devine, after all."

Michael grinned. "Do you really mean that, Annie?"

"More than you'll ever know, I'd be so delighted if you wanted to do it. Do you?"

"I've always wanted to, ever since I was a kid," Michael confessed. "But I knew you were next in line, so I put it out of my mind. When Bull asked me to help out yesterday I loved it." He smiled shyly, color flooding his face. "Who knew I was such a romantic, huh?"

"Who indeed," she teased. "Will you take it on?"

Michael stood up and leant over to kiss her cheek. "I'd be honored."

"Let's tell Da. He can announce it in his speech." She tapped her father's shoulder to quietly get his attention. Smiled apologetically at his audience. "Excuse me everyone, I just need to talk to my father for a minute." Her heart soared. At last, she was rid of her unwanted inheritance.

"JACK! YOU'RE HERE!" Noel thumped Jack heartily on the back.

"Meet Annabel." He introduced a small, pretty blonde who smiled shyly next to him, his arm draped over her shoulders. "You haven't met yet, but you organized our first date."

"Hi, Annabel." He put out his hand but she ignored it, stepping closer and leaning up to plant a kiss on his cheek.

"We're better friends that that, Jack." A smile lit up her face. "You helped us find each other. Like Cupid. You're a friend for life."

She snaked her arm around Noel again,

smiling up into his face with a look of such devotion and love an ache tore at Jack's chest.

"It worked, then," he forced out.

"It certainly did." Noel held up his girlfriend's hand, revealing a diamond solitaire. "Annabel and I are getting married."

"That's great!" Jack shook Noel's hand, genuinely glad someone, at least, had managed to find their happy ending.

"Everyone has been saying it's too quick," Noel confessed. "But you know what it's like when you find the woman you want to spend your entire life with, you just know, so what's the point in waiting? Sure, we don't know everything there is to know about each other, it's only been a few days after all, but we know what matters."

"We know we love each other." Annabel flushed red. "We have all the time in the world to find out the rest."

"I'm glad for you." Was it that simple? Jack's eyes searched for Annie in the crowd.

Noel leant forward and whispered in Jack's ear. "Annie's in the back, at the matchmaking table with her father, she's been checking out the door for the past hour."

"Thanks, Noel." Jack patted him on the back and strode to the table, unable to see Annie or her father through the crowd of people. Determination gave his steps purpose.

She might not know it. She might not even agree, but before the night was out, she was going to admit she loved him. And more, if he had his way. He was halfway there when Bull stood up, with Niall beside him, holding a microphone.

"Ladies and gentlemen, I give you our matchmakers, Bull Devine!" There was a deafening roar of approval followed by clapping. Jack edged closer. "And this year, helping Bull out because of illness, we had Annie Devine." Annie stood, as the crowd continued to cheer, "Michael Devine," Michael stood, waving to the crowd and hamming it up for all he was worth, "and Jack Miller. Is Jack in here somewhere?"

Jack raised his arm high, catching Niall's eye. "There he is! Let Jack through to the matchmaking table, everyone!"

The crowd parted obediently. Jack made it to Annie's side. She had done something different with her hair, pinned it up. She smiled up at him radiantly. *Of course.* They were pretending to be in love until after the festival. He braced himself for a chaste kiss.

She reached out to him wordlessly, and, heaven help him, he forgot about the pretence of being her boyfriend, and kissed her hard, reaching for the nape of her neck and pulling her close. Her mouth opened under his and she kissed him passionately, to the delight of the crowd.

"Love is in the air this year folks." Niall laughed as they eased reluctantly apart. Jack slid an arm around her waist and held on for dear life. She might not want to spend the rest of her life with him, but he wouldn't give up without a fight. Not after she'd kissed him like that.

"Speech!" the crowd roared.

Bull accepted the microphone. "I missed being here with you on the first couple of days. The first time I've missed any part of the festival in the forty years I've been your matchmaker. Thank God, I was lucky enough to have some excellent helpers. They went through the book with me. Together we made some excellent matches."

"So, I'd like to thank them. Firstly, my daughter, Annie, who left Dublin and came back the moment I needed her." Annie bowed. "If there's anyone left who hasn't heard the news, Annie has won the Chocolate Oscar competition. Now she can open her chocolate shop in Dublin." The crowd erupted, many people working their way directly to Annie to congratulate her.

"I'd also like to thank Jack Miller," he continued once the excitement had died down a little. "Lightning diverted Jack from his route, and brought him here to us. I like to think Durna was really his intended target, even though he didn't know it. He's shown himself to be a wonderful matchmaker, full of understanding and compassion."

Warmth flooded Jack's face. He looked out at the nodding faces of the crowd. Many of the familiar faces raised their glasses. He'd never been at the receiving end of such warm praise before.

"He might have been born far away, but he belongs here. I reckon he's an honorary Durnaman." The crowd obviously agreed, clapping and shouting their approval.

"Finally I'd like to thank my nephew, Michael. He volunteered his help for the last few days. I know all of you who know Michael were delighted to see him in the matchmaking booth." He grinned at Michael's embarrassment. "As you know, I matched Michael nine years ago with his lovely wife, Grainne."

Grainne blew Michael a kiss. He theatrically blew it back, to the crowd's delight.

"Michael found love for himself. This year he's helped find it for others. I'd like to thank him, and I know all of you would like to thank him, too." Bull turned to Annie, Jack, and Michael in turn. "Would any of you like to say something?"

"I would." Annie voice was clear and strong. She accepted the microphone from her father and brought it to her mouth. Jack was loosening his grip. She held on tightly. "It's great to be here everyone," she started, smiling around the room.

"And I'm so glad my father is better and taking the reins again. Being the matchmaker is a difficult job!"

"You're going to have to get used to it, honey!" a woman called from the back of the room, and Annie shook her head grinning widely. "Hi, Carly." She greeted her friend with a wave. "That's one of the things I wanted to talk about." She glanced at her cousin before continuing. "One day my father will decide it's time for him to step down. Hopefully not for many years."

She took a deep breath, and squeezed Jack's hand harder. "But when he does, I'd like to let you all know he has a very worthy successor. My cousin Michael is going to be the next Devine matchmaker."

There was a stunned silence at her bombshell. Everyone stared. A muscle worked in the corner of her jaw, and she swallowed. "I know it was expected I'd take on the job when my father retires. I've thought about it a lot over the years. This festival has really brought home to me how important it is that the matchmaker has a talent for it. I did my best, but without my father, I would have been terrible at it." She grinned.

"Michael is an heir to the matchmaking legacy, too. He's also passionate about it, with a natural aptitude. Michael and I have discussed it, and I'm pleased to announce he would love the role."

A murmur of conversation started up. People were nodding. Understanding. *How could she have thought they wouldn't?*

"I'd like to thank you all for your support over the past few years. I know you've all been looking out for me." She glanced down, overcome with emotion.

"Good on ya, Annie!" someone shouted. The room burst into applause again.

Jack squeezed her hand tightly. "You don't need to say any more," he whispered, and somehow she made out his words in the din.

"Oh, I'm not finished yet." She brought the microphone up to her lips again. "I just have one other thing to say." The crowd quieted, every eye in the place glued to her face. "Two years ago I stood up in the church to tell you all my wedding was off. It was the most difficult thing I've ever had to do. I felt I was different from everyone else, marked out. I didn't handle the aftermath well. I told myself I was unlucky in love. In my embarrassment, I felt everyone must see me as a failure. Now, with different eyes," she slanted a look Jack's direction. "I know I was wrong. You've all shown me that."

She turned to Jack, facing him bravely while her fingers squeezed his painfully. "Now, here, in the presence of my family and this bar room congregation, I'd like to declare publicly I've fallen in love with Jack Miller. I hope to hell he loves me back, or I'm going to die with embarrassment." Her entire body was so tense vibrations of her shivers telegraphed through their entwined hands.

Jack took the microphone, his eyes never leaving hers. "You couldn't pull me aside and tell me this privately?"

Annie shook her head.

Jack pulled a small box out of his pocket. "I had a plan for this evening." He turned and spoke the room. "Something important to tell Annie. And something important to ask her." He held up the box and the room erupted. He held his hands up, there was more. "But I guess, as we're among friends." He sank down onto one knee. The crowd hushed in expectation.

"I love you, Annie. I don't care where I live, as long as it's with you." Her eyes glistened with unshed tears, her dimples telegraphing to all and sundry that they were happy ones. "Well? Are you going to marry me or what?"

"Yes."

He stood up and gathered her into his arms again, and the matchmaking festival celebrated another match.

AFTERWORD

I hope you enjoyed this book. I have many other books available in large print for you to enjoy, do check them all out!

Word-of-mouth is crucial for any author to succeed. If you enjoyed the book, please consider leaving a review at Amazon, even if it's only a line or two; it would make all the difference and would be very much appreciated!

Printed in Great Britain
by Amazon